M000306515

Chinese Checkers:
Three Fictions

Chinese Checkers:
Three Fictions

Mario Bellatin

English Versions by Cooper Renner

RAVENNA PRESS
2006

Ravenna Press

www.ravennapress.com

Foreword

by Ken Sparling

"Because he is not you"

The poet, M. Sarki, says you might love a writer simply because he is not you.

Mario Bellatin is not me and I am not Mario Bellatin. Nor am I Cooper Renner, the man who translated these works by Bellatin. This is important. But more important, I think: Cooper Renner is not Mario Bellatin.

So what is Renner's job as translator of Bellatin? Is it his job to render Bellatin's variously occurring meanings as the text progresses? Certainly, I would guess, Renner must begin by stumbling through the text, plucking out meanings individually and probably mostly out of context. A word, a phrase, a sentence, a paragraph. And then the next. And the next.

But then, when he reaches the end, Renner goes back to see what he has done. And what has he done? He has committed a sort of violence, no doubt. Perhaps a violence akin to what Bellatin perpetuated himself when he excavated his narrators' thoughts and pasted them onto paper in Spanish.

So Renner must return to the scene of the crime and what must he do now as he surveys the chaos that violence invariably generates? Must Renner now find within the chaos something to hook the various meanings together? Could we call that something Bellatin's intent? Is Renner, as he revisits the carnage he has wreaked, hunting for Bellatin's intent? Could we say this? What more could we say? Is there more?

Does Renner leave behind something of himself when he translates the text? Does translation leave in the wake of its carnage bits of Renner, as well as bits of Bellatin? What is Renner to do with these bits of himself as he encounters them upon revisiting the scene of the crime?

Could we say that the intention to translate is an act that veils itself within the text? Is it something available for unveiling by the reader? Should it be? In other words, in reading the translated text is the reader encountering Bellatin alone, or Bellatin and Renner together?

It seems too obvious that Renner will leave something of himself in the translation, no matter what his own intention. The more interesting question might be: should Renner be afraid of what he might leave behind, as though his intention to translate were a weapon that he must do his best to conceal or dispose of as he revisits the text and finds himself in the middle of the chaos engendered by his crime?

Is it frightening to translate? If so, does bravery involve feigning fearlessness in the face of translation; or does true bravery require the admission of fear even in the march forward through the text? Should Renner's fear show itself in the text?

Maybe we could use this problem—this idea that translation might be frightening—as a place to begin to think what Bellatin might have hoped to unveil in writing his story in the first place. What was Bellatin hoping to translate and how frightening must that be? If Renner used Bellatin's Spanish rendition as a map to help him translate into English the mind of the boy whose mother put his genitals on display at the baths, what would Bellatin have used to map out this uncharted territory?

When a writer excels in his use of language; when he's written and written and written; when he's rewritten and rewritten and rewritten; when he's had the advice of editors and friends and professionals and relatives and strangers; when the jagged edges of his writing begin to disappear—disguised, banished, eliminated, killed by his aptitude—and the story moves cleanly through the words so that the words, and the writer, are forgotten, and the work the writer did to create the story is lost in the seamlessness of the work, the translator arrives and must resurrect the violence. As Renner sets out to translate, he encounters Bellatin's story piece by single piece. And now Renner must decide whether or not he wishes somehow to salvage within his translation the sudden encounter between one section of the text and the next—an encounter that may not have been available in the original text. And if Renner decides not to salvage this adventure of stepping through the text piece by piece, he must find a way to smooth the text in the translated version. In so doing, wouldn't the translator have to consider straying from the literal meaning of the original text in attempting to translate?

Are we, readers of this English translation of a Spanish translation of the thoughts of a character in a book, translators ourselves? Are we here to re-encounter the violence of translation as we encounter the violence encountered by the translator, who himself encountered the violence of the writer translating a story out of air?

How does one translate what is inside the mind? How does Bellatin get what is in his mind into language and onto a page? How does Bellatin get inside his character's mind and come back with what he found and take it and give it language and put that language down onto paper? Does Bellatin shape what he finds in the mind to make it fit a story? Does this shaping of thoughts–this decision to include or exclude, to smooth or ruffle, to fragment or to mould–call for discipline of some sort? Is this discipline a friend or an enemy to the thoughts that precede translation?

At one point in one of Bellatin's stories, "My Skin Luminous", Renner renders Bellatin's rendering of his narrator thus: "It no longer matters to me to know any other details. . . ."

Within Bellatin's decisions about what matters here, and Renner's decisions about how to honour Bellatin's decisions, is it possible to see what really matters, what might really matter to me? Is it possible to agree together, Bellatin, Renner and me, on what really matters? We began by loving each other because we are not each other. How will we end?

I have learned nothing more of my father, although surely he would have appreciated like no one else my lamps covered with soap suds. – from "My Skin Luminous" by Mario Bellatin, as translated by Cooper Renner.

It isn't just Renner's translation. Renner's translation no doubt produces a certain dis-ease in the reader. But the dis-ease Renner produces must mirror the dis-ease Bellatin feels in encountering his narrator's thoughts. What of the narrator, though? He seems to feel no real dis-ease with his situation. He seems almost entirely comfortable displaying his genitals for his mother's gain.

Here is how Renner translates one of Bellatin's sentences: "I have no doubt that she will act with the decisiveness characteristic of her."

It could have been translated otherwise. For example: "I have no doubt that she will act with her characteristic decisiveness."

Does this alternate translation sound cleaner? More familiar? Somehow better? Maybe even more correct?

Does this sentence arrive as it arrives because of Renner's translation? Or does it arrive as it arrives because of Bellatin's original composition? Either way, it does arrive as a moment slightly askew. Not askew within the context of the story, for the story itself seems askew. No, this sentence comes as slightly askew in the moment it is experienced as a sentence read.

This sentence mirrors the askewity of the story. And whoever is doing it, Renner or Bellatin, the text renews itself continually, one unexpected, slightly askew moment after another.

Would rearranging this sentence fix anything for the reader? How would it be better to let the reader slip through the text unaware of the translator's struggle?

Renner's translation might be seen as a mismanagement of sorts. As a betrayal, perhaps. A betrayal of clean, well-ordered English, in favour of… what? In favour of something that Bellatin arouses in him? A betrayal in the name of a loyalty, as all betrayals must be. So what is it Renner winds up being loyal to? What in Bellatin inspires loyalty?

I think Renner is loyal to the track Bellatin's narrator tramps through his life as he has resurrected it in his mind. The narrator speaks rationally, cleanly, carefully, with a sense of precision and progression. But the life he describes is not rational, clean, precise or progressive. The narrator seems to miss the life lived cleanly, the way Tom Waits or Bob Dylan miss. Bellatin's narrator's thoughts fumble forward through Bellatin's precision and Renner captures this sense of fumbling in his translation.

I say Renner's translation falls short of the clean, journalistic writing we've grown accustomed to. Renner's translation retains something of the monumental struggle to make meaning that writing always contains, but too often hides. I believe Renner is loyal to the struggle and thus does not hide it.

You stand a chance, here, in reading this translation of Bellatin, to hear the anguish behind and between the words set down by Renner as he hikes through Bellatin's arrangement in search of something more than simple translation—in search, I believe, of meaning.

Toronto, Ontario
January 2006

Chinese Checkers

. . . and so they are also forced to deliver
the dead bodies to their fathers.
Greenhouse Effect,
Mario Bellatin

1.

Every time I enter the examination room, I put the same questions to myself. Looking at the metal table with the metal straps hanging at the sides makes me wonder if I am really interested in seeing the dozen patients who fill the office every day. The constant dealing with women seems to have altered my character. I feel that touching their bodies only for medical reasons deforms, in some way, my desires. And yet I do not understand why, at my age, I need so much to hurry to massage parlors, nor why I stop the car when I see a girl walking through some dark part of the city. They rarely pay any attention to me although on occasion they agree to get into the car and go for a drive. Usually I take them for a drink somewhere discreet, or park my car at the shore. Those encounters usually end up in one of the motels that rent their rooms by the hour. I never take anyone to the office: the clinical smell and the memory of the medical situations which have developed there negate from the outset any kind of excitement. For that reason as well I have ignored the hints dropped by patients. Likewise that of a nurse who spoke to me of indecent things only days after having been employed. I dismissed her before she finished her first week on the job. I prefer anonymous experiences. All are simply adventures which last a very short time. Almost always they take place after I leave the office. Others occur in the early hours of the afternoon. I cannot get carried away and forget the time. Even though my wife is not fastidious about my schedule, I do not want her to begin to harbor any suspicions about my behavior.

It has been a long time since I stopped asking myself how I really feel about my wife. It seems that I am too accustomed to her presence. I believe that, when we married, I did not calculate how much age matters. My wife is two years older, a fact of no importance when one is young. Only when she began to bear and raise our children did the years that separate us become apparent. At some gatherings I have told other men about my adventures on the street. At first they listened to me; some even asked me for details. For some time now, however, I have noticed that they avoid the subject. Many, I know, had one experience or another long ago. Now they seem to prefer the peace of the home. In the winter they host luncheons for their children and grandchildren. In the summer they often spend the weekends at their beach houses without much thought about anything happening in the outside world. My wife and I lead such a life together, although in the first years of our marriage we tried to establish a more worldly pattern. We bought our first house, for example, because the entertainment suite was quite attractive. There were two spacious living rooms and a terrace overlooking a well-tended garden. It did not matter to us that the bedrooms were rather uncomfortable or that we would have no privacy ourselves once the children were born. In those years we dedicated a good part of our time to planning cocktail and other parties.

When my wife became pregnant, our routine suffered somewhat, but immediately after our daughter was born we put her in the care of a qualified nanny.

I had two children, one of whom is dead. The older wed an industrious young man who seems to be satisfied with the marriage. For their part, they have two children, making me a grandfather. In spite of appearances, however, I see that my daughter is not content with the way things stand. A good deal of the time I sense her agitation. I do not believe that anyone else notices. Perhaps I am the only one. Perhaps I owe that perception to the years in my profession, to the fact of having seen women's reactions in various circumstances. When I diagnose the lump in the breast as possibly malignant, when I advise an operation, or when I indicate that the baby-to-come may have a difficult birth, I face responses which would leave the mouths of others hanging open. I do not believe my daughter can do much to remedy the situation. Perhaps it helps her to focus on the rearing of her children. I know also that she sets aside the time to take a photography class. She has even taken some shots of me. In one of them, I have on the white jacket I wear when I am seeing patients. As a whole, my daughter has provided me with any number of felicities, but I find it difficult to speak of my younger child. I do not know what happened as he grew up. Perhaps I did not pay attention to the symptoms which began to appear when he was still an adolescent. I remember how he began showing up at home with bruises on his body. Perhaps a wound to the forehead, a scratch on the arm or a noticeable limp.

I achieved financial security fairly quickly. Besides my private practice, I also opened an office after a while with other doctors. We founded a clinic together. During that time we moved to another house. A neighborhood of a better class, more isolated, suited us. It was my wife who took care of the details. The new house was so big that each member of the family had his own quarters. My wife decorated a living area where my children could entertain their friends. They were both entering adolescence at the time, and I believe that the events which shaped their characters occurred inside those walls. Everything seemed to be going well, although I had already begun, a while earlier, to feel that I was suffering a sort of professional crisis. When I was a student, medicine had absorbed all of my time. My greatest desire, in those days, was to be able to practice my profession without distraction. I think it important to point out that I am illegitimate. My mother had a severe nature and my father, a well-known doctor, was for his part married to a woman who had borne him three children. Perhaps in order to prove that neither she nor I were beneath anyone, my mother devoted all her energy to securing my future. She enrolled me in prestigious schools and worried about every aspect of my university studies. It was my mother who established me in my first office. That merely began the ascent. Next was the advantageous marriage I had contracted: my wife belonged to an important family. The climb continued when I moved my practice into more expensive accommodations. That came after the purchase of our first house and other such steps. But until that moment my vocation as a doctor was most important to me. Neither my marriage nor the birth of my daughter could compete with the satisfaction of helping a woman give birth or of performing surgery on a patient. Something, however, changed suddenly. At a specific moment I no longer wanted to advance. It happened precisely when my colleagues suggesting founding a clinic. For whatever reason I started to think that further advancement would put my vocation in danger. I remember that, at the time, my wife and I were enjoying a vacation. We were visiting the largest Caribbean islands. I believe that seeing how my wife enjoyed that cruise made me forget my desire to hold to everything I had acquired to that point. Upon our return I immediately signed the contract with the other doctors.

In this way I initiated another stage of my career. It is true that my first sense of vocation had diminished, but in spite of everything I found my duties a constant challenge. During that period my son was born, I took part in various conventions abroad, and the entire family enjoyed a vacation trip. This pattern continued even as my children grew. But I was no longer interested in my career as a quest which had to continue reaching new heights. I noticed, with a sort of panic, that I had begun to practice medicine in an almost mechanical manner. With some effort I managed to repress the fear which this situation began to cause me. From that moment forward, I continued as though I were truly committed to each case that came before me. That attitude did not simply give me a certain sense of calm; it also, strangely, led me to become preoccupied with the external self I presented. Soon the only thing that really mattered to me was aging. I took note of it not only in myself. The constant presence of my wife was also there to remind me that I was not a young man. I began to take special care in my dress. In those years fashion was going through significant changes. I was tempted to follow the new trends strictly, but my way of life prevented me from moving too far from a rather classic style. I let my sideburns lengthen and adopted the wearing of whites and pastels. One event strikes me as particularly disagreeable, something which happened during a baptism my wife and I had been invited to. It was Saturday. In those days I went to the clinic in the mornings to check up on the condition of patients staying there. That morning I had to perform a minor procedure on a woman who had recently been operated on. As it was a simple matter, I did not change my clothes to attend her. When we arrived at the baptism, a friend of my wife pointed out a small spot of blood showing on the white slacks I was wearing for the occasion. I tried to dismiss the matter as of no importance, but my wife's friend continued to worry about the wound she supposed I had suffered on my leg. She seemed to be incapable of connecting my profession and the spot. Many of the guests had noticed the spot, and I am sure that most of them understood the truth immediately.

In those years my life was reduced to my daily attendance at the clinic or my office. It was then I had my first adventure. It took place with a woman I encountered in front of the parking lot of the building I worked in. My office is situated in a modern structure where the most prestigious doctors in the city practice. It features large windows of polarized glass which permit me to watch, from my desk, the sun setting on the horizon. There are several areas. I make use of a smaller room for minor procedures. As usual, that day I remained at the office until 8 p.m. I had dealt with nothing out of the ordinary. That day had not distinguished itself from hundreds of afternoons in which I saw one patient after another. I recall having seen two pregnant women, another woman who needed her IUD changed, and three whose visits were for routine examinations. I was walking to my car when I saw the woman, standing next to a lamp-post. I was thinking of nothing when I approached her. I greeted her with fear. She told me we should leave together. I wanted to accept immediately, but I could not allow the parking attendant to see us. I told her she should wait for me on the next corner. While I started the car, I questioned what I should do next. Just then I remembered a boy, not terribly old. I had seen that boy the week before, when he and his mother had hurried to the office. The boy's mother had to see me regularly. She always brought her son with her. My nurse performed the treatment the patient needed. I had to watch, however, in case any complication occurred. On this occasion the boy was seated, as usual, on the black leather sofa I keep between the waiting room and my office. While the nurse prepared the woman for her treatment, I sat next to the boy. The treatment would last at least an hour. The boy knew it. I believe that is why he told me a long and complicated story of which I understood very little.

I listened to the boy's tale, perhaps because it was the easiest way to fill that dead space produced in the consultation. I listened until the nurse appeared and told me that the patient had tolerated the treatment without problem. I left the boy seated on the sofa and went to examine the mother. That night, lying in bed next to my wife, I thought again about the story I had heard in my office. Only then did I take note that the boy's head did not have the customary roundness. At almost the same instant I forgot everything and fell asleep. The image of the boy and the story he had told returned to me only when I was in my car about to turn on the engine. As I started it up, I hoped that the woman would not be awaiting me at the next corner. It was possible that another driver had already picked her up. But there she was, in a yellow skirt and a purse, decorated with gems, hanging at the shoulder. Everything happened in a matter of seconds. I stopped the car, the woman got in, and we moved on. I still remember the sharp thump of the door closing. When I returned home that night, my own wife had supper ready. It was late. The whole family, however, had been waiting for me before sitting down to eat. It occurred to me that it might be a special day. By the uneasiness on the faces of my wife and daughter, I knew that something was going on. My son apparently had no knowledge of the situation because he began eating with his usual indifference. My wife did not speak until dessert. My daughter was going to be engaged in just a few days. After dinner they told me that the preparations for the ceremony were almost finished.

I believe it was only after the marriage that my wife and I realized the depth of the problem with our son. As the only child still at home, his presence was more evident. Discreetly I discussed the matter, over the telephone, with colleagues. No one had a clear idea about how to approach the issue. I recall making the calls during my daughter's honeymoon. I remember the time because it was during those days that I carried, in the pocket of the robe I wore, a postcard the newlyweds had sent us. That evening I had my second serendipitous encounter with a woman. At that point I had no experience with what was going on in the streets. For that reason I rushed to one of the many massage parlors which advertised in the newspapers. I knew that those parlors were secretly brothels, but that was the first time I had confirmed it. In making my selection I was guided solely by the name. After having visited several of them, I know that I was lucky on that occasion. It was a discreet place, clean, with a young and friendly personnel. I would have liked to become an occasional customer. It was not possible because those places, fearing the police, close their doors with some regularity. It bothers me also to have relations with the same woman twice. As a consequence I now combine visits to the salons with encounters on the street. I also frequent several houses which require an appointment. To this point I have had no serious problem, except for the woman who secured my telephone number and address.

I never learned how she managed to find them out. She was a woman I picked up on the street. Perhaps she found one of my business cards in the car. I went with her to a deserted beach. Not one which couples generally visit. Her company had given me a certain sense of confidence. Our discourse was not, for that reason, confined to the sexual. We spoke as well of other things. I chose that beach because at others I had had annoying experiences with people who like to spy upon parked cars. The woman may have searched the interior of my car when I got out to buy the cans of beer she asked for, or perhaps the card slipped out of my pocket. She called the office, threatening to speak to my wife if I didn't give her a certain amount of money. I let her continue without responding. Then I hung up and told the nurse that she was not to disturb me with any other calls that day. I never heard from her again. I do not know if, at some point, she carried through with her threat. If so, my wife has never let on. I remained nervous, although not particularly because of the blackmail itself. What worried me was not knowing how thoroughly I would be able to manage the situations my behavior was beginning to create. I remember thinking at that moment about the story the boy in my office had told me. Only then did the absurdity of the tale strike me. It was obvious that he had invented the story. The boy's demeanor did not really surprise me, and so I had not, until then, doubted the veracity of what he had told me.

The day of the blackmail attempt I went home in a bad humor. I had no desire to see anyone. Most assuredly my wife would await me with the table set. My son, by the same token, would not be there. He had adopted the custom of leaving before I arrived home. I believe that his habit improved things for all of us. He assumed this custom after a particular incident in which I was involved. It began early one morning when someone rang the doorbell insistently. The night before I had come home early from the office. Before going to bed, I watched the news and then read a couple of chapters from a book that had just been published. Sleep overtook me with the book in my hands. I felt it only distantly when my wife took it from me and then turned out the light. The doorbell woke me. Over the intercom a voice told me that my son was in trouble. I needed to go to the police station immediately. I had thought my son was in his room, although I do not recall having seen him come in the night before. I considered it likely that he had done so after I had fallen asleep. When I went to his room, I found the bed made. Weak rays of sunlight fell over the diamond-patterned quilt. That morning I learned that my son had made unauthorized use of a stolen credit card. In the days to come I went to a great deal of trouble to secure his freedom. When he came home after three days, I noticed that he was at pains to make sure that we saw each other at little as possible.

I do not want to make any particular testimony in this regard, but I have noticed that my state of mind often influences my work as a professional. I remember that at the same time I began to doubt my vocation there was a series of deaths in cases under my care. Of course there was no direct relation. Although, to be sure, there was some degree of negligence on my part. The first victim was a mother in labor. At the moment of birth it was difficult to know if the baby was not in the correct position, although if I had been more careful I would have ordered exams prior to the patient's entry into the delivery room. The child died as well. Another case even more clearly could not be held against me. Death was caused in this instance by a tumor which had been diagnosed as malignant from the beginning. Later there was the patient who committed suicide after her sterility was confirmed by the exams which I ordered. It is evident that I bore a major responsibility in no case. But inside I felt a certain guilt. As if the energy generated by my state of mind attracted evil toward the women who frequented my practice. It soothes my conscience somewhat to think of the miraculous cure of the same woman whose son spoke to me that day in the office. That occurrence helps me balance out, in some fashion, the ledger of my professional obligations. The boy's mother had been diagnosed with a cancer with complications. Thus the frequency of her visits. She had to undergo a round of chemotherapy. As I indicated, she invariably brought her son with her. It seemed that, with such a serious diagnosis hanging over her, she did not want to be separated from him even for a moment. In one of those many visits, I do not remember exactly which, the boy was sitting next to me again. But on that occasion he did not utter a word. He had spoken to me only the one time. The fact of our being together again, however, made me remember once more the details of the story I had heard weeks earlier.

I do not remember at what point the nurse interrupted that long discourse. Nor do I know how the boy managed to tell me all of it in such a constricted period of time. I do not believe I have added anything from my imagination. I remember the white-garbed figure of the nurse leaving the anteroom with the rubber gloves already on. The nurse and I left the boy alone and closed the door. The patient lay on the metal table. She was covered with a lightweight robe. I noted that the thick hair of a few weeks earlier had thinned. The color of her skin had darkened to an ashy tone. Her eyes were closed. A metal rack stood in one corner; from it hung the bottle of serum which had just been administered to her. When I came up to the table, the nurse carefully brought up the cart with my instruments. I began to palpate the torso. As my hands were examining her, the patient on a few occasions complained. By that time the tumor had reached a considerable size. It was her first examination after the initial treatment. I noticed, however, that in spite of her physical condition her willpower was not diminishing in any significant way. She put forth an effort to seem animated. While she awaited her appointment, she customarily told stories to her little boy. Two months later, the tumor began to shrink. Some weeks beyond that, it disappeared completely. When I could no longer feel it, I ordered new tests. The results were negative. I even made a small exploratory entry to be sure. Shortly thereafter, I declared her cured, and since that time she comes in only sporadically for checkups. As before, the boy always accompanies her.

That is one of the cures I consider miraculous. These usually are a matter of textbook cases with all of the characteristics required for a stereotypical development. But for some reason, which I feel sure that none of my colleagues has yet managed to puzzle out, the ailing bodies, on certain occasions, demonstrate completely unexpected symptoms of improvement. As for the boy's mother, the growth of the tumor had even affected several organs. It is possible that some people consider these recoveries normal and any ineptitude as originating in medical science. Especially those who see medicine as an activity sustained in charlatanry. In some ways I agree with those ideas. I confess that there are hundreds of functions of the body which are totally mysterious to us. But in the matter of miraculous cures things are different. I use this term for the recoveries which take place when, after years of experience with similar diagnoses, I see conditions which escape the normal flow of things. When one of these situations presents itself, I have a reaction which I cannot describe with precision. The comparison seems rather unlikely, but the sensation is like that produced when I meet with a woman of the streets.

It begins with a feeling in the throat. My mouth goes dry, even as my hands begin to perspire in an abnormal way. Sometimes I even feel a slight cramping in my legs. In that moment I can do nothing to turn myself back from the actions I am about to take. If I am driving I stop the car. If I happen to be in a salon I tell them to end the massage immediately. The first time I visited what was in no uncertain terms a brothel, that feeling took hold of me as soon as I entered. I believe that the scent floating in the air was of great importance. My sense of smell told me that something decisive was going to happen. I experienced, quite forcefully, that sensation in the throat. The dryness in my mouth was not at all ordinary. While I climbed the stairs that led to the rooms I began to feel the moisture on my palms. Seeing that long hall, with the women awaiting me in front of their doors, I had to stop for some moments. Minutes passed before I regained my equilibrium. I continued walking. I accepted the first woman who offered herself to me. I returned to the place a number of times. I went until I had tried almost every woman who worked there. In order to do so I had to excuse myself from home with stories of imaginary patients and fictitious surgeries. But as my visits increased, the sensations in the throat, the hands and the legs began to decrease. The last time it was like going into my own home. For that reason I looked for other establishments. I tried out several addresses near the port. The first incursions were perfect. I entered places where the low level of the light made seeing almost impossible. Everything was in shadows. It was hardly possible to intuit the bodies reclining in the salons or the small rooms where the women received their clients. I knew that almost all of the customers were Slavic and Asian sailors. The smells and noises there were more penetrating than in the businesses I had patronized earlier. Every woman had a transistor radio which she kept on at all times with the volume as low as possible. I know there are brothels of even less standing, but I would not want to fall into the temptation to visit them.

As I returned home after those visits, I thought sometimes of my son's unusual conduct. From the first I aimed to remain inflexible in the face of his behavior. Such an attitude was, I believe, a response to the manner in which I perceived life in those days. Now, on the other hand, I am able to understand the existence of a certain type of degradation which might have served to help me learn earlier how to be a better father. Among things even worse, I know of men who make women beat them or ask them to urinate on their backs. All of this I have heard through the improvised wooden partitions which often separate the small spaces. Once a woman asked me to do strange things to her with one foot. I remember when I rushed off, still in my bathrobe, to pick up my son from the police station where he was being kept. I saw, in the other detainees there, characteristics which reminded me of men at the brothels. I consider them servants of a dark place which, I would like to believe, neither my son nor I were obligated to frequent. But, although the circumstances were different, both of us seemed destined to observe closely a facet of life which very few truly come to know. Even so, in spite of beginning to sense all of this, I never wavered in my intransigence in our day-to-day relations. The reason might be that, as long as he was alive, my son was becoming a greater problem every day. Not simply for himself, but also, more importantly, for others. Although my wife tried to hide it from me, I know that she too faced difficult situations. One morning when I returned home unexpectedly because I had forgotten my medicine kit, I found my son just coming in from a night away and thuggishly demanding money before leaving again. I would have preferred not to witness the scene. I immediately put my hand into my pocket and put a number of bills into my wife's hands. Then I went up to the second floor to retrieve the forgotten kit.

I do not understand why precisely now I remember one incident in particular. About the time I turned fifty, I began to spend time with a new group of friends. The way they carried themselves and approached life made me think about the possibility of taking on behaviors outside my routine. Not unlike what happened when I started to feel that I was aging and wanted to change my manner of dress. I recall one member of the group especially, who had at hand an appreciable fortune. That character seem to be excessively interested in my family. Besides talking to me on the telephone daily, he regularly sent flowers and chocolates to my wife and daughter. At that time my daughter had just finished high school. She was not certain about the direction her life should take. This man often invited us to parties he held in a house on the outskirts of the city. At those parties I usually let myself go into a sea of sensations. I let the music and the marijuana take over my feelings. As regards the marijuana, I had my doubts at first, though after a couple of parties I smoked it like all the other guests. I even tried out hashish in a pipe made in the Orient. My wife was obviously somewhat disoriented at these gatherings. She spoke excessively to the first person standing in front of her. One of the parties hosted by that man, whom I certainly never saw again, ended with a rather peculiar situation. Most of us guests were in the living room when suddenly my daughter appeared with her face bathed in tears. Seeing her the other guests froze for a moment, although just a few minutes later everyone had returned to what they were doing before. The only point of discord was my daughter, whom my wife was comforting. I put on the jacket which I had left at the entryway when we arrived. I knew it was time to go home. I went to the two of them, put my arms around them, and we left the house without saying goodbye to anyone.

Another special memory of my children is of the afternoon I took them to the zoo. I was alone with the two of them. Although our children never made any demands in this respect, we had never allowed the presence of domestic animals in the house. On that visit my children were dazzled by the number of cages. What I had planned as an hour's stroll became a trek that lasted until the zoo closed. I established that day, for the first time, that my children had different tastes. While my daughter inclined toward the birds, the reptiles seemed to appeal to my son. I realized as well that they were brave. They had no fear of putting their small hands between the bars. It is true that we were among the cages of the harmless animals, but they had no way of knowing that. I bought several packages of special food, sold there at the zoo, which they gave repeatedly to the elephants and monkeys. On the way home they never stopped talking about what they had seen that day. When we arrived, they told my wife all of the details. They talked about the animals' shapes, about the sounds they produced. They gave her a description as well of the way the cages were laid out. In the days to come they continued referring to the zoo with the same eagerness. For some reason I paid attention to those recountings and was able to note, with a kind of sadness, how their enthusiasm waned slowly with the passing of time. One day, suddenly, it completely vanished. They never mentioned our visit again and never asked me to take them back. Such indifference came to affect me. I did not, however, want to get involved. I never mentioned the matter. I recall that a number of images from that visit came to mind at certain points during the story that the boy in my office was telling me.

When the boy finished relating the story, I fixed my eyes on the sofa where he was sitting. The color had been selected by my wife who, as usual, had been careful of that purchase in every way. When we acquired it, we visited several shops until we found what she had in mind to buy. As a rule my wife gives herself over in that way to her daily activities. I do not know if she does so in order to feel safe in playing an established role or if she truly feels that she must carry her duties through to the end. For example, besides her usual routine she sets aside one day a week to work as a volunteer at the hospital where I have privileges. On those days she works with great intensity with the nurses in the ward for the burn patients. She also takes charge of the Christmas celebration in my clinic. Last year she had the idea of making a living nativity using the administrative employees as actors. Without anyone's noticing it, she had made, over the course of the months, a series of visits in order to select secretly those who would play the various parts. She always carried a notebook in which she recorded the results of her investigations. Sometimes at night I saw her going over her notes and changing one name for another. At the end of September she revealed her choices. She had to persuade those who did not wish to take part. Only when she had secured the participation of everyone did she begin rehearsals. Earlier she had told them that she had reserved for herself the role of the archangel Gabriel. She even had his costume ready. She had ordered it made by her trusted tailor, who had prepared for her a pair of wings which moved thanks to a mechanism attached to her right pinkie finger. From one of the interior windows of the clinic I took to watching my wife while she directed the rehearsals. She was apparently demanding: she energetically admonished any actor who was not performing satisfactorily in his role. My wife was not the only member of my family involved in the project. She took advantage of the classes my daughter was enrolled in to ask her to take some photos. Her job was not limited simply to taking portraits of the nativity scene when it was ready, but also to making a graphic history of the entire process. Once the presentation was over, my wife kept the photos in an album and promised me that she would not repeat, in the coming year, several small errors which, she assured me, had been made.

That performance was one of the pleasant things we shared at Christmas. My wife and I had dinner alone on Christmas Eve. My daughter, her husband and my grandchildren had to eat with my in-laws. For his part my son did not put in an appearance during the holidays. His absence meant, in some way, the lifting of a burden. I believe I would not have had the strength to tolerate, in his presence, the exchange of feelings one prefers at that time of year. At midnight we embraced. Friends called on the telephone. After supper we went to bed. Before that we gave each other our gifts. My wife had asked me for a piece of jewelry which she herself had selected excitedly, and I received a pair of ties, just as she had given to me every year. I slept deeply that night. Oddly I did not rise until almost mid-morning. Since my youth I have not been a late sleeper. My body was accustomed to being up and about before seven a.m. I was a bit startled to see how bright was the light coming in the window. My wife was already downstairs. I ought to have gone to the clinic to check on a few patients, but a feeling of pleasure kept me at home. After a shower I called the office to let them know I was not coming in. I asked them to inform me of any development. Wearing only my bathrobe I went into the music room. On one of my last trips, I had purchased a record with a special selection of mambos. I put it on and surrendered myself to music I had listened to on so many occasions. At that moment my wife came in with a tray. I noticed her good mood. She attempted several dance steps and asked me, nostalgically, if I remembered those days when we had parties almost every weekend. I told her yes. But I added, a little insensitively, that I no longer missed that way of life. After I had listened to the music for about an hour, my wife interrupted the session by telling me that I ought to get dressed because my daughter and her family would be arriving soon to celebrate with us. I stood up, turned off the stereo, and went upstairs. I chose a yellow sport shirt with white stripes, beige pants, and sky-blue tennis shoes.

It surprises me that I have just made such a detailed description of my attire. As a young man I paid almost no attention to what I was wearing. It was my mother, whose tastes were rather spartan, who decided what I would wear. Oddly enough, the boy who told me the story in my office also wore sky-blue shoes. At a certain point he brought them up onto the sofa. I noticed that they were athletic shoes. One had come untied. When he lowered them to the floor, they left tracks on the black surface of the sofa. I do not know if those tracks had begun to acquire some significance in my head, but I decided to get rid of the sofa a week after proclaiming the boy's mother cured. It had been about ten years since I had purchased it. That seemed to me a long enough life for any piece of furniture. I let my wife know how I felt. She agreed. She added that she would take care of its disposal tomorrow, as long as I did not want to keep it until I had a new one. It would have been more reasonable to wait, but my wife knew my intransigence after making any decision. She suspected that I could not stand the sofa for another day. When I asked her what she would do with it, she replied that she would think about it later. Not that I want to appear tight-fisted, but the leather was still in rather good condition. Most likely my wife would give it to the first person inclined to accept it. To one of the house cleaners, or to a nurse who worked in the burn ward at the hospital. At that time I was still visiting a brothel on a detour off the highway. The madam would have been happy to have that sofa. It could well be used there. The furniture was rather past its prime. Although, perhaps, it would not have been a good idea to offer a gift of such value in that sort of place. They might begin then to charge more for their services than before. I suspected just that, since it was obvious to me that those women could use more money. They not only required payment in advance, something which had never happened in the massage parlors, but also had, on several occasions, taken advantage of my carelessness and gone through my pockets. At least I am usually at pains, before patronizing one of their services, to establish the price precisely. It is also my custom to keep a limited amount of money on hand, which they can freely steal from me. Apart from the sensation in the throat and the legs, another thing I have noticed during my secretive visits to those houses is an increasing need to smoke. Tobacco has never been my vice. In fact at one time in my life I refused it openly, and on the handful of occasions when I used marijuana I had serious problems with the smoke.

In fact it would have pleased me to bestow that sofa upon any of the madams I knew. Although I would not have known which deserved it most. I have mentioned that I thought of giving it to the matron of the brothel I was frequenting at that time. But other than its being the place I spent several hours a week during those days, there was no reason for it to have been chosen. In most brothels I have been treated well. Although on occasion I have experienced encounters one might call brusque. I am fifty-eight years old, I have lost some hair, gained some weight, and have behaved discreetly. I do not know if it is my age or my appearance which makes the people who work in those places respect me as they do. But once, I believe it was this past winter, a substantial altercation almost took place. I had arrived at a house located in a neighborhood near the cemeteries of the city. As usual I had little time. I had arranged with the madam to have a different woman at each appointment. The first time I visited any brothel I assured the madam that I would come often as long as she reserved an opening for me in the early afternoon. By doing so, I could leave my wife after our lunch and then return to my office by sunset. Thus I could count on an hour or two in which my actual whereabouts would be a mystery. The afternoon of the incident I arrived at three. The madam received me and immediately led me to a rear yard where two prefabricated rooms had been put up. Before going, she asked me to relax. The woman she had chosen would appear shortly. I sat on the narrow bed and reached for my cigarettes. They had spread only a single sheet on the mattress. I smelled it and ascertained that it was clean. When I looked carefully at what had been done to the room, I realized that the madam had gone to some effort to receive me.

In one corner of the room, I found a basin full of water and a half-used piece of soap next to it. There was also a small towel and a roll of toilet paper. I was preparing to undress when I heard people coming near. They seemed to be arguing. I could distinguish a man's voice and a woman's. Also the madam's voice. The man was making threats which were soon mixed with obscenities. I got up quickly from the bed. Once on my feet, I put out my cigarette and straightened my tie. Then I put on the jacket which I had kept over my arm the whole time. I was afraid. What was happening outside seemed to be a situation which I could not control. I remained immobile next to the door, attentive to developing events. The three people continued arguing in the yard, just in front of the room I was in. Apparently the man was the woman's husband and he had just discovered the sort of activities his wife was engaged in. The woman was crying, denying that she was a prostitute, and asking the matron to defend her. Strangely, the argument suddenly ended. There was an immediate, absolute silence. Then I heard a rumor of voices, but at a considerable distance. Five minutes later, the madam opened the door to tell me not to worry, that it had been a matter of no importance. She added that the woman would not be long in appearing. While she was speaking, she came into the room to make sure that everything was in order. She checked the basin, the soap, the towel and the toilet paper. She moved them, putting them in the same arrangement but in another corner. Then she told me to take off my jacket and lie down. Shortly after she left the room, the promised woman came in. In spite of the disturbance, she was making the effort to appear pleased. As she began to open her blouse, I noticed that her lips were trembling and her hands moving nervously. Even so she fought to maintain a smile. I could not tolerate the situation. I put on my jacket again and, with no remorse, left the room in silence.

As I drove to the office, I could see through the windshield of the car how the city's appearance changed the farther I left behind the neighborhood where the brothel was located. Despite the sordidness of the incident, it occurred to me that there had been something luminous in the woman's attempt to disguise the situation. She seemed to be an expert in that kind of behavior. The tremor in her lips and the somewhat nervous movement of her hands might even have been taken as manifestations of some degree of sexual arousal. Perhaps that is why I refused her, because I am too accustomed to women who badly perform the roles they want to play. I see those characteristics all the time in the women who come to my office, in my daughter when she makes an effort to hide her unhappiness, and in my wife's attempts to make it seem that our life together is completely normal.

After the occasion in which I was forced to take notice of my son's demands for money from my wife, there began, curiously, a period of relative calm in the house. Once this time ended, however, I became aware of something disturbing which my wife had been keeping quiet. My son had discovered the combination to the safe in which we keep the jewelry. I believe I have not yet mentioned that my wife has a special love for jewelry. Not so much in showing it off as in the manners of obtaining it. She often employs uncommon methods in its acquisition. She spends entire mornings in the booths at the suburban markets. She often finds real jewels among a welter of artificial pieces. Over the years she has learned a series of ways in which to recognize an authentic piece immediately. She even uses a jeweler's lens which she carries with her when she embarks on her expeditions. When my son secured the combination, the number of jewels in storage began obviously to decrease. Only when their disappearance become more than blatant did my wife refer to the matter. She did so during one of the breakfasts we like to take together. It was summer. I remember it because the table had been set in the garden. In a roundabout manner she told me that she could not explain how several pieces had gone missing. She added that she had said nothing because she might have been mistaken. But by that time she was sure that there had been no error. She said nothing more. Neither did she expect a reply. We continued eating. We did so in silence. That morning, from the clinic, I called several colleagues to ask for their help. I thought that perhaps they would already be able to respond positively. It was possible that methodologies had advanced in that field. But as I feared, they gave me no hope. They told me that various types of treatment had been developed, though none was entirely effective. They explained them to me. It was as they had said: not one completely convinced me. It seemed most appropriate that my son spend a period of time in a sanatorium. I proposed to undertake what was necessary, although at last I did nothing concrete. I resolved that farther along, when the situation was truly insupportable, I would take action.

I am sure that my wife never shared with anyone how tense the situation was in the house. I do not believe that even our daughter would have known the whole truth. To a point I agree with the approach my wife took. I think that our daughter had enough on her hands with her own household affairs and did not need anything else to worry about. Although it is possible that one of the reasons my wife kept quiet was the reaction our son-in-law might have. After seeing his behavior when our son died, I grant that my wife made the correct choice. My daughter was rather distraught over the death. That made me think that my children had been closer than I had supposed. I had glimpsed something in the visit we made to the zoo, but I had not observed on any other occasion a more than usual degree of attachment. Strangely the crisis which the death of her brother produced in my daughter was not evident until a month after his burial. She had a sort of breakdown which led to her admittance to a rest clinic. Her husband came to see me, calling upon me as a doctor. He asked me if my daughter's condition might not bear some resemblance to her brother's problem. He seemed frightened. Perhaps he was afraid he would lose his wife. Or maybe he thought that the family's heredity was going to be characterized by a sequence of abnormal behaviors. I do not know how much he will have been told about the life and death of my son. In any event, I managed to calm him down. Officially my son's demise was considered the result of an inability to tolerate the substances which he had administered to himself. In other words, it was labeled an overdose. My son-in-law's intellect seems to have developed solely for money-making. It strikes me that he has an innate sense for sniffing out where he ought to make investments and reap significant profits. It astonishes me how, year after year, his economic situation markedly improves. But despite the fact that my daughter seems to have everything, I repeat that I note in her a powerful dissatisfaction. Otherwise I do not understand why she refused the trip her husband suggested just after she left the rest clinic. The idea was to forget the bad memories and to share a second honeymoon. My daughter flatly refused to take part in that trip. Her excuse was that she had lost too many hours from her photography class. There is no doubt that she had taken a great liking to the camera. But such does not seem to be a motive for refusing a proposal such as my son-in-law had made. With respect to her fondness for photography, she has even asked me to allow her to take some shots during a birth. I still have not answered her, I suppose because the thought of her presence in the delivery room while I am working seems too disagreeable to me.

I remember clearly the afternoon my son died. I was in the office attending an older patient who had the beginnings of an infection. I prescribed antibiotics. I remember the prescription well, because I took the call from my wife while I was writing it. I was alarmed because my wife knows how much I dislike being interrupted at work. The nurse is also aware of it, but calls from home are not subject to her disposition. When I answered, I heard the anguish in her voice. She told me it was an emergency, that our son had taken sick and that she needed me at home immediately. After hanging up, I attempted to show no signs of worry in front of the patient. I continued with the visit as if nothing had happened. I finished the prescription and then explained the regimen she had to follow. When the woman left the room, I called the nurse to let her know that I had to leave the clinic for a while. I asked her to inform the patients still in the waiting room. Anyone to whom it was convenient could make an appointment for another day, although no one was likely to want to wait. I asked her also to prepare my doctor's bag. I left my office jacket in the adjoining room and put on the tobacco-colored coat I had chosen to wear that day. I arrived home a half hour later. I parked the car behind my wife's car. At one time I had also bought my son a car, which I sold after the unpleasant episode at the police station. My wife was clearly awaiting my arrival. I had hardly turned the engine off when she came outside. She was pallid, and her movements betrayed her distress. Seeing her I realized that anything might have happened. She quickly told me that our son had come home in a calamitous state. Besides several tears in his clothing, there were bruises on his face. He was completely out of himself and had not stopped asking for money. My wife had given him some, but our son had demanded more.

In the face of my wife's inability to satisfy him, he had begun to destroy everything he found in front of him. Decorations and some of the windows that overlooked the garden. He shattered the screen of the television in the room my wife had decorated for our children to entertain their guests. When I arrived he was shut up in his room, where apparently he had continued with his destruction. For a while now he had been calm. Or at least my wife had heard nothing new. I put my arm around her. In that way, together, we entered the house. I saw that the damage had really been significant. I recognized the remains of ceramic pieces from the entryway. A number of paintings had been ripped from the wall and thrown to the floor. I continued my path to the bedroom. I opened the door without knocking. Except for when I had been called to the police station, I had never entered his room in that way. I found my son, surrounded by chaos, sitting in the corner. He looked pitiable. He clung to a fistful of money. I believe he did not recognize me; otherwise he would not have held out the money and asked me to help him to leave the house. I slowly drew closer. I did not want to upset him. I believe I spoke to him. Something about not worrying, that I was there to help him. I went down on my knees at his side, but he showed no perceptible reaction. He seemed not to feel my presence. I was able then to open my medicine bag easily and prepare a syringe with a sedative. Given the circumstances, I believed it appropriate to inject him with a larger dose than normal. To my surprise, my son began to respond in a way opposite to what I expected. He started to show signs of distress. He tried to jerk away the arm I was injecting the drug into. I had to hold it forcefully. Shortly thereafter he went into convulsions. I moved back a short distance and saw how my son's body was shaking in a rhythmic way. My first reaction was to wrap the syringe and the empty vials in paper. Then I put them away in my bag.

The funeral service was discreet. Other than my wife, no one seemed to reveal any genuine pain. As I indicated, a month passed before my daughter showed how truly affected she was. The body remained all day at a funeral home in the neighborhood. An hour after his demise, when I had still been engaged with the mortuary in arranging the details of the funeral, I began to realize with astonishment that my wife was struggling not to break into tears. I noted as well that she was beginning to gather up, angrily, the various objects our son had destroyed shortly before. It seemed to be a matter of restoring order, in any way possible, to the house. Our daughter, who had arrived after I called to relay the news, helped her. Fifteen days after the burial my wife had the idea of replacing the shattered decorations. Thus she spent the greater part of that time in a series of specialty shops. She called me at noon one day. I was in the office at the time. Not long after my son's death I decided to suspend for a while some of my professional activities, although I treated, from time to time, important cases. My wife called from a shop which sold only wedding presents. She was having a problem with her credit card. I came to the shop to resolve the issue personally. When, from a distance, I spotted my wife there, I stopped for a moment to observe her without her knowledge. We were in a large, well-lit store. The floors were white, and they were immaculate. Seeing my wife dressed in mourning made an impression upon me. But contrary to what I might have supposed, I found her rejuvenated. Several days after the interment, she had visited a beauty salon where she had asked them to even out the cut of her hair and to dye it dark blonde. I do not know if she suspected what actually happened in our son's room. When I left it, I told her that his weakened body had not tolerated the dose of sedative I had just given him. Immediately she began to weep tears which seemed very bitter to me.

I consoled her until she suddenly stopped weeping. She moved then from my side and accused me of being the only guilty party. Her recriminations included the claim that I had always acted as if I were a god. I do not know what she meant by that. Perhaps she suspected that I had intentionally caused that death. An accusation of that sort could have proved horrific. I have not spoken of the matter with anyone. At first unwanted ideas arose to trouble me. That continued until recently. I attributed them to the state of tension I had had to endure from the day of the death. But since those ideas ceased, I feel a comforting inner peace most of the time. Then my wife turned back, with an unusual, light pace, to our son's room. I remained in the room where our children had entertained their friends. The employees of the funeral home would arrive shortly. From outside I heard my wife speaking to our son as though he were still alive. She spoke affectionately, just as she had fussed over him when he was a small boy. When she left off speaking, she began to tidy up the chaos, unable to restrain her tears. As soon as she saw me in the shop, she came to me with the credit card in her hand. After various negotiations, the problem was resolved. I stayed with her a half hour longer. Once she had finished with her purchases, she suggested we go together to a restaurant. I refused the invitation. My excuse was a patient in a delicate state. I do not know why I lied. To be honest I had nothing I had to do, and it would not have displeased me to go to a restaurant in her company. I had, besides, the afternoon free. As I said, I had taken a break from my practice in token of mourning. During exactly that period, the patient who had been miraculously cured called me. It was time for one of her visits to ascertain that her health was still sound. When I was taking the call, the physical image of that woman, as well as that of the boy with the somewhat abnormal head who always accompanied her, came to me. After listening to her speak, I decided to direct her to a colleague I trust. I heard nothing more of her. As I indicated, I had no plans for that afternoon. However, perhaps to attenuate the lie I had just told my wife, I ended up spending the rest of the day at a brothel which, at that time, I had just discovered.

2.

The boy told me, there in the office, that a few days earlier he had spent the weekend at an uncle's house. The house is located in a small city next to the sea. At one point, a messenger knocked at the door and, strangely, left an envelope addressed to his father. It surprised the boy that such a delivery would have been made to the wrong address. He took it, even so. The dispatcher had sent it from the same city. Before leaving, the messenger gave the boy a note which informed him that a part of the shipping charge was being returned because the delivery had taken too long to arrive. The boy carefully read the contents of the note. Then he asked the messenger to explain certain details. The matter concerned the dispatcher's modern system of delivery which reimbursed a certain percentage of the cost of the service if delivery was delayed. The amount, which awaited disposal in the company's central office, was written on the paper. As it was an amount not to be ignored, the boy immediately went to his uncle to tell him what had happened. He had his doubts about doing so because he imagined that the grown-ups would not allow him to collect the money. Such had happened to him already on other occasions. His parents received the prize which he won when he unwrapped a candy with a winning ticket inside. Likewise the monetary compensation that belonged to him for finding a fly in a soft drink bottle he had not yet opened. Even so he hurried to his uncle who, after listening to his account, looked over the delivery. Then, with his red ink pen, he began adding up figures on the envelope. To make his work more efficient, he asked the boy to bring him the calculator he kept in his desk. The uncle seemed to want his calculations to be perfect. He said there were always surprises in these payments. Surely they would deduct this or that tax from the amount given, or unexpected expenses. To tell the truth, he said that the amount the boy had thought to receive would be a long way from what they would actually give him.

Staring at his athletic shoes, the boy told me it had bothered him deeply that his uncle had marked up the envelope. He was embarrassed about what they would think at the dispatch office when they saw the figures in red handwriting. He tried to stop the uncle from continuing, but the uncle insisted on it. He filled the envelope with numbers, some of them incorrect, with the corrected figures on top of them. When the pen ran out of ink, the uncle had to get another. Now the ink was not red, but black. Before returning the envelope to him, the uncle looked over the attached note again and noticed a fundamental fact. He pointed out that the money could only be recovered the same day that the envelope was received. It was Saturday. Worse, the sun was already going down. It might not be possible to collect anything. The boy went to the telephone and picked up the directory. He looked for the company's number. He found it. But when he lifted the receiver, he heard that someone was already speaking on the other line. He went to the yard to waste time. He came back. He lifted the receiver again.

The conversation continued. He began to mourn silently. He walked through part of the house to waste more time. He went up to the roof and walked around the whole thing several times. When he lifted the receiver again, he thought the line was free but, after a brief silence, he heard a woman's voice. He did not know whose voice it was. It had to be someone in his uncle's family. Although it could also be the voice of a neighbor whose phone was out of service and had asked the favor of using the telephone there. The boy felt that he was being made fun of when that voice ordered him to hang up at once.

Without looking away from his shoes, the boy told me he cried. He did it in secret. He went to the yard and hid in a small shrine where there was a Virgin dressed in a sky-blue habit. He tried to communicate with her, to ask her help in securing the money the agency promised. After half an hour he went back inside. Seeing him in such a state, one of the family members asked him if something had happened. The boy told him then how badly he needed to use the telephone. The relative told him about some public telephones which were being installed in the city. He warned him that they did not work with coins, but rather with plastic cards. Quite near the house, on the sea-wall of one beach which was full of people in the summer in spite of the choppy water, they had put in several of those booths. The relative suggested that he use one of the bicycles in the garage in order to get to one of those phones as soon as possible. He even wrote down on a piece of paper the number of the delivery company, which for some reason he knew by memory. The boy took the bicycle. The house was located in a neighborhood where there was a big park with a lot of trees planted in straight rows, which gave the park a geometric look.

When the boy left the house, the afternoon was advanced. The sun continued its decline, giving ruddy touches to the atmosphere.

The boy indicated that he had just arrived at the beach when he saw, far off, the booths they had recommended to him. They were painted a light yellow. The boy saw that, as always, the sea was choppy. Tall waves struck the shore. The sky was cloudless so that he could see the sunset in all its splendor. He looked over the sea-wall a couple of times. The chrome of the bicycle shone as he pedaled. Finally he decided to make his call from the farthest booth. He left the bicycle secured to a light post. He had already gotten one of the required cards from a shop. He punched the numbers without taking his eyes off the bicycle. He did not have to wait long before the telephone was answered. It was a male voice that responded. The boy told him his situation. The voice at the other end told him that he knew nothing about that offer. The boy insisted. The man suggested that he come to the office to discuss the matter face to face. He told him they were open until eight p.m. After hanging up, the boy approached the sea-wall. He stood there a moment looking at the sea. Then he moved toward the beach. There were still sunbathers at that hour. There were even umbrellas up here and there. The boy walked across the sand and came to the waterline. Since he was still wearing his shoes, he could not get his feet wet. He retraced his steps to the bicycle. He took off the lock, got on and began the ride back to the city. The man he had talked to had given him the address of the office he needed to get to.

The boy arrived shortly at one of the busiest streets of the little city. He was careful with the traffic. The main office occupied the first two floors of a modern building. Through the plate-glass windows one could see the employees working, wearing blue and red uniforms. The boy did not want simply to leave the bicycle locked to a post. He was suspicious because there were so many people in the street. For that reason he pedaled vigorously back to his uncle's house. He had decided to leave the bicycle and come back on foot. His uncle's house was not far. But when he knocked on the door, no one answered. He stood at the front door for ten minutes. He rang the bell several times and there was no response. He thought about climbing the wall, but instantly surrendered any such idea. At last he decided to leave the bicycle hidden in the bushes that grew in the outer yard. He was careful that the branches not scratch the paint. He was at pains as well to make sure that no one would notice the hiding place. Then he walked slowly to the dispatcher. He was two blocks away when a car stopped next to him. It was his uncle, asking him to get in. The uncle owned a sports car. The boy got in and told his uncle the outcome of his activities. The uncle listened in silence, but became alarmed when the boy mentioned leaving the bicycle hidden in the bushes. The car had been heading toward the delivery business but suddenly made a turn in the opposite direction.

The boy told me that the posts and the trees along the street passed by them at an increasing speed. Before arriving at their destination, they almost had an accident. The uncle crossed a major avenue without paying attention to the stop signal. At that moment a bus full of passengers was coming down that road. The squeal of the brakes frightened the boy, who curled up in his seat with his fingers over his eyes. The uncle sped up to avoid the collision. They kept going without another mishap. Stopped in front of the house, the first thing the uncle did was head for the bushes the boy had pointed out. He pushed them aside and found the bicycle exactly as it had been hidden. The uncle entered the house, holding the bicycle by the handlebars. The boy remained, for a few moments, alone at the entrance. He thought then that perhaps the negotiations at the dispatcher would be easier if he took with him the envelope addressed in his father's name. He had only just realized that he did not even have with him the note which explained the money to be returned to him. He went into the house and shortly thereafter came out with the envelope and the note. He walked about fifteen blocks. When he arrived at the office, he recognized through the big windows the employees in their uniforms. His first action was to speak with the receptionist. He explained the situation to him. The man replied that he did not know that the company offered such a service. He suggested that the boy discuss it further with one of the employees at one of the windows. The boy had to get into a line. He stood behind an old woman in rather unusual clothing. She wore a dress, cinched at the waist, whose cloth threw a red shine. She had a fox-skin over her shoulders. She had also made up a complicated hairdo adorned with a metal crown. Her shoes had spike heels, but no backs. It occurred to the boy to compare the old woman to the Virgin whom he had visited at his uncle's house before leaving. He noticed features in common with the image, to which he had prayed while the stranger spoke on the telephone. After waiting several minutes, the boy touched the old woman's back and told her about her resemblance to the Virgin in the shrine. The old woman looked at him for a moment before answering. A bit upset, she informed him that she did not appreciate such a comparison. She added that she despised a religion in which the central idea concerned a father who condemned his son to be murdered. Seeing the old woman's reaction, the boy asked her directly if she knew about the company's offer to refund money if a delivery was delayed. The old woman's expression became calm again, and she replied that she knew nothing about that. She recommended that he verify it from a public telephone before wasting more time in the line. The boy told her that he had already done so. He gave her the details of his visit to the beach. The old woman seemed interested in the existence of those telephone booths. She asked him to tell her exactly where they could be found. When the boy did so, the old woman pointed out that, some years earlier, in that same spot there had been a broad terrace where she used to spend the summer.

The old woman told the boy that the terrace had been constructed over some stakes which went into the sea. At that time there were quite a few umbrellas, all painted white, that the vacationers rented for their enjoyment while looking out at the bay. According to the lateness of the season or the hour of the day, the umbrellas were easily moved. In one corner there had been a bar. At the front were several small steps for going down to bathe in the sea, though always while holding onto a rope. Entrance to the terrace was prohibited for children under age five. On one occasion, however, a woman secretly brought in her two-and-a-half-year-old daughter. The woman made herself comfortable under an umbrella, while her daughter went to play where the terrace formed a number of overhangs. The irresponsible woman claimed that the child was well mannered and could be left to herself for long periods. No one knows what the girl was doing during this time, playing or making mischief. The fact is that she fell into the water without anyone's notice. The mother realized minutes later that she had disappeared. Some vacationers congregated around the desperate mother who was, at the time, looking at the sea and shouting for the girl. The managers of the terrace immediately hired several fishermen whose boats were anchored in a nearby inlet. The mother remained there all night awaiting news. She leaned against the railing while the fishermen agitated the waves. The woman's husband arrived shortly after being told of the tragedy. The lifeless body was found the following morning. The sea returned it when the first rays of sunlight were showing. From then on, the number of vacationers dropped notably. Two years later, however, the event seemed to be forgotten. Even so, at that time certain stories about the dead girl began to circulate. It was asserted that, during the night, she appeared on the terrace. It was also said that the mother had gone insane. They said that she had started complaining that she had no one to play Chinese checkers with in the afternoons, a passion which, until then, no one had known she had. After she finished telling the story, the old woman with the crown confided in the boy that she had never been able to have children. That was the real reason why it had bothered her to be confused with the Virgin. And that was the reason as well why she could not imagine the torment the woman had gone through, which had driven her into the insanity everyone talked about. Without leaving his place in line, the boy imagined the old woman giving a bottle to a baby just a few months old. He drove that image away to focus on the service windows. The employees continued to be very busy.

The old woman with the crown apparently did not have enough patience to wait for the line to move forward. She gave up, leaving the boy in the last spot. As the boy would learn later, her chauffeur was waiting for her at the door. The old woman got quickly into the car. They pulled away immediately. As soon as the vehicle neared the front of the house where she lived, the automatic garage door went up. Inside, two assistants were awaiting her. They delicately removed the fox-skin. Seeing how tired she was, they told her that it had been crazy for her to have attempted taking care of her activities by herself. That was what the chauffeur was for. The old woman had gone to collect a shipment of seeds which had been sent to her from the capital almost a year ago. She did not reply to her assistants' recriminations and went to the covered patio she owned. Without changing clothes she asked them to bring her gardening tools. The assistants appeared with scissors, some wire, and a big rubber water hose. The old woman remained there until night fell. She looked at her watch and saw that it was nearly eight. She thought that, just then, the businesses would be in the process of closing their doors to the public. By now it would already have been decided if the boy she had met had been able to reach his goal. From her yard the old woman could not know that it had occurred to the boy, right after she had gotten out of the line, to ask to speak to the manager. He ascertained that the greater part of the officers worked on the second floor. The problem he faced was going up without the requisite permission. The entrance to the staircase was closely monitored. Anyone would have thought it led to an office dedicated to confidential matters. The boy understood that it was impossible to return to the receptionist he had spoken with when he arrived, because that man already knew that he was trying to obtain a reimbursement from the company. He looked the layout over and understood quickly that that employee had been placed so that he could control everything without needing to move from his chair. If the old woman had not gone a few moments earlier, the boy might have asked her to help him. But despite it all, the boy was able to get the better even of such vigilance. He slipped through, thanks to the customer who was at the front of the line and who began speaking in a loud voice. It seemed that the delivery fees had gone up the day before and the customer had only the exact amount necessary to send his package. He claimed that they had not warned him before, because he had now foolish ly lost very precious time standing in line. The employees tried to calm him, but he was exasperated and not listening to them. Finally the receptionist had to intervene. The boy took advantage of the opportunity to put the stairs to use.

The boy confessed to me that he climbed the stairs, thinking about what it would mean to a loving father to lose a child. He was upset about the story the old woman had just told him. From the time he was just a few months old, his father often took him to the beach. For most of those visits, they had been accompanied by the very same uncle in whose house the boy had received the delivery in his father's name. On one occasion the father and the uncle took advantage of their visit to fish from a rock. The boy had to sit on the sand and wait for them. There was something special about the scene. The rock they had chosen to fish from was completely round. Besides that, its whiteness contrasted with the green of the sea. The beach where the boy waited was small. It was really just a nook between two promontories. The father and the uncle moved away with their fishing tackle. They climbed the rock without difficulty. The boy had brought a sand sieve. Just as his father had suggested, he began to play where the sand was dry. He never got close to the water. It seemed that no one, however, had taken the tide into account. Two hours later the water began to advance. The boy got wet in the water timidly approaching the area where he was playing. The boy wanted to stand up and run. But the water continued to advance. Meanwhile the father and the uncle gave up fishing because they had not caught anything. They got ready to go back. The father looked toward the sea while he reeled in his line. He saw then the boy's plastic sieve, floating at the current's mercy. He immediately threw down his fishing gear and ran furiously toward the beach. With the water halfway up his legs, the father picked up the boy with both arms. It was then that the boy began to cry.

Looking at her watch, the old woman was already tired of the chores she had been tending to. She went into the house after leaving a mess of the tools she had been using. She asked her assistants to collect them. She then called the delivery company on the telephone. The telephone was answered after several rings. She was told first that the company had just closed, but that they could take care of any immediate need. The old woman then asked if they offered reimbursement for the delayed delivery of a package. After a delay of several seconds, they told her that a matter of such a nature could only be dealt with personally. They invited her to come to the office on Monday to resolve the matter. Leaving the telephone off the hook, the old woman turned then toward the garage to look for the chauffeur. She ordered him to take her once again to the dispatcher's office. The chauffeur told her that it might be closed already, and that it was unlikely anyway that the seeds had been delivered that day. The old woman did not answer. She said loudly that the affair of the seeds was not what concerned her. She asked the assistants to bring her the fox-skin which she had worn that afternoon. After putting the fox-skin on her, the two women spent a few minutes tidying her dress. Because of her work in the garden, she had gotten the dress rather dirty. The old woman completely ignored their suggestion that she wash her hands. She seemed anxious to get into the car which the chauffeur had just backed out of the garage. The chauffeur drove on streets with less traffic. For that reason the drive went quickly. When they arrived, however, the lights at the delivery office were already turned off. The old woman got out of the car as soon as it was stopped. She approached the windows. She put her face to the glass and looked inside. Suddenly a hand touched her shoulder. The old woman turned around and faced the boy from the line.

The boy wanted to speak but the old woman covered his mouth. Then she immediately took her hands away and showed them to him, telling him everything she had done since leaving him. Then she took his arm and took him to the car. The chauffeur opened the door, and the boy got in, followed by the woman. Once they were seated, the woman adjusted her crown. Then she ordered the chauffeur to take a stroll. She told him not to return in less than an hour. The boy began an examination of the car's interior. He set to one side the envelope and the note he had brought with him. The seats were soft. Both the window controls and the door-locks were automatic. When the chauffeur disappeared, the old woman told the boy that she had never gone back to the terrace where she had always spent the summer. Over the course of the years, the summer sun had damaged her skin, and so she had chosen to engage in other sorts of activities. She had begun to take an interest in indoor gardening, a fairly uncommon practice chiefly because of the amount of electricity required for it. She appreciated the beauty that flowers were capable of offering if they were well protected from the weather--saved, to be sure, from the savage rays of the sun which gave them all the typical look of the flowers everyone was familiar with. In the beginning, it cost her a good deal of effort to learn a series of secrets which became quite useful. A number of times she had to await the change of the seasons in order to discover the alterations the climate brought about in closed spaces. That period lasted about three years. She knew it because there were three winters which killed her plants. That time is fading in her memory. She sees through a fog a series of employees installing hundreds of powerful lights. She cannot produce an exact chronology of the happenings of that time. Among other things, she does not know during which stage of her apprenticeship, of her preparation of gardens partially subterranean, she was taken to a mental health center. There she met other mothers with whom she carried on more than one conversation. They were accustomed to sitting together in a dining room with several tables. But things were not completely harmonious in that place. There were times when the patients fought over any imaginable foolishness. At times the problem was a stolen sweet or refusing to take one's midday pills. When they behaved really badly, they were threatened with seclusion in a room which few knew and which they called the Klino. In that period the old woman with the crown was not greatly worried about the gardens which they wanted to put at her disposal in the sanatorium. They were outdoor gardens with the usual lawn and colorful flowers. The old woman preferred, during those days, to talk with the other women patients. One of them was an artistic virtuoso. For that reason she always carried with her a portfolio of white pages; she also had a wooden box full of watercolors. That woman spent most of her time portraying the patients. She deceived them. She told them she was going to take their picture, but in reality she painted them with an astonishing rapidity. In less than two minutes she was ready with any portrait. Most of the patients hung them over the heads of their beds. The virtuoso also sang and played the guitar. There was always a circle around her, listening to her. At first no one knew the songs she performed. But little by little they all learned them to perfection. In that way the afternoon sometimes passed with astonishing speed. At twilight they had to return to the ward and get ready for bed.

The old woman came back home after three months in the sanatorium. In her absence, the husband had moved out of the house. Before doing so, he hired the current assistants. The chauffeur remained loyal to his long-time post despite the circumstances. The husband visited her from time to time, especially when the old woman had to take to her bed because of the recurrence of her nervous condition. That pattern continued for several years, until the summer morning when they told her that her husband had died in his sleep. The old woman explained to the boy that it grieved her that his death had caused her neither true sadness, nor the recurrence of her feelings when the girl drowned in the sea. Suddenly the boy ceased examining the interior of the car and turned on the small ceiling light. He stared at it fixedly. The old woman's crown continued to rest exactly in the middle of her hair.

The fox-skin, on the other hand, had slipped to one side. Without looking away from the light, the boy told her that the people at the dispatcher were not going to pay him what he was owed. He had gone up to the main offices where a subordinate employee had attended to him and had explained that there was indeed such a promotional offer. It had been designed to attract new customers, but it had not yet gone into effect. The envelope which had arrived at his uncle's house was a mistake, sent too early. The primary reason the promotion had not yet been launched was that the company had not decided if the remittance should go to the sender or the receiver. The business had already received telephone calls asking for a clarification, but the boy was the first person to visit the office in person. The old woman wanted to console him, telling him not to worry, that all would be resolved if he would come with her to her house. There she was going to show him the garden. Then she herself would give him the amount of money promised. She would also prepare something for supper and, if he liked, he could remain for the night. She explained that, as she had never had children, she had placed her emphasis on the section of her house meant for entertaining. It had sizeable rooms and terraces which overlooked the immense garden. Because it was quite an old house which had been adapted with certain modern elements, neither the bathrooms nor the kitchen were in keeping with the rest of the house. They were nothing but little rooms with tiny windows.

The boy told me that the house of the old woman with the crown was not unpleasant. He took a look at the living room and the dining room before going to the garden. The old woman had gone in before him. She told him about each plant and how she had to tend them. They remained there about an hour. One of the assistants interrupted them in order to let them know that dinner was served. They entered the dining room, where a long table covered with a white cloth awaited them. There were only two chairs, placed at the ends. The assistants positioned themselves behind the chairs. The old woman walked resolutely to her place. The assistant at that chair helped her seat herself. The boy turned to the other end. He sat and opened the napkin to place it over his knees. The old woman looked at him from her place. The metal crown continued to preside over her hair. The fox-skin lay yet across her shoulders. The assistants left and, a few minutes later, returned carrying small silver trays with two finger-bowls. The old woman badly needed to wash her hands. She moved the bowl to one side, however, and gave herself over to watching the boy as he tidied up. Astonishing everyone, the boy did so correctly. While they ate, the old woman gave the boy a sort of test concerning the plants he had just learned about. She questioned him primarily about their names and the methods of caring for them. After the boy replied correctly, the old woman began to describe other places where she used to spend the summer. She had not only frequented the terrace where the girl drowned. Once she had traveled by boat with her husband to spend the season on the beaches of another city. The journey was not very long. They were on ship for three days. They embarked on a ship of great draught which even carried cattle in its hold. The second morning on board, when the passengers were on deck enjoying the sun and the ocean breeze, one of the sailors cried on the portside that two of the cows had fallen overboard. Most of the passengers hurried to the railings to look over at the cows in the middle of the sea. They were more or less ten meters from the ship. They swam by moving their hind legs rapidly. Some of the passengers suggested that the ship stop to rescue them. No one paid them any mind. The spectacle lasted about fifteen minutes. By that time the cows were no more than two specks in the distance, and no one dared to speak. Furthermore most of them had already stopped watching. The old woman with the crown said that the last to leave the railings were herself and her husband.

The old woman waited until the boy finished his dessert to tell him that she would show him his rooms. The boy replied that he still had not decided whether to stay the night there. Besides, he had to ask permission. By this time they would be worried about his absence. He was obliged to call his uncle to let him know where he was. The old woman told him he certainly would not. She added that it was already decided that he would stay over. She had given instructions to the assistants as well as the chauffeur that it would be so. The boy was alarmed; he stood from the table and turned toward the door to the street. The assistants caught him, taking him securely by the arms. They carried him to the second floor. His shouts meant nothing. The assistants were strong enough to control him without difficulty. Holding him even more tightly, they put him into one of the rooms. It was a room decorated with a little girl in mind. There were dolls of various sizes and also a large number of stuffed animals. In the middle of the room there was a bronze bed from whose canopy hung pink tulles. In a corner were the envelope and the note which he had left on the seat of the car. The assistants locked the door. The boy at first had no idea what to do. Then he went to the window. He wanted to open it, but it was obvious that it was secured.

The boy paced the room while asking them out loud to release him. After an hour, the old woman opened the door. She had changed her clothes. The skin which now covered her shoulders was white. The silk of the dress was entirely unreflective. The crown was also different. It was no longer a metal crown but one that seemed to be made of a synthetic material. She carried a small serving dish with a glass of milk and some vanilla cookies. The boy did not wait for the old woman to take more than a step inside the room. He ran into her, knocking her to the floor. The old woman fell on her back. She remained motionless while the milk dripped between the boards and the cookies lay scattered about. The crown rolled to a stop at the side of a child-sized doll. The boy ran for the street. He met up with neither of the assistants nor with the chauffeur. The house was completely silent. He went down the stairs, came to the vestibule, and opened the front door. He was surprised that it needed no key. The night offered itself in all its fulness to him. The boy ran the first blocks. Then he adopted a calmer pace. When he had still quite a distance to go, he realized that a car was approaching at great speed and then was stopping next to him. It was the old woman's black car. The doors opened rapidly, and the assistants and the chauffeur got out of it. The boy was about to run, but the chauffeur ordered him to stop. The boy confessed his fear to me. He obeyed at once. The chauffeur came up to him with the envelope and the note, which he had left forgotten in the room. Then he gave him the amount of money the old woman had promised. Then the assistants and the chauffeur got into the car and drove away.

The boy kept walking, holding the envelope, the note and the money the chauffeur had given him. He had to

cover about thirty blocks to arrive at his destination. At
last he saw his uncle's house. Dawn was already near. He
did not know if he should knock on the door or wait until
it was truly morning to do so. He was afraid that, if he
woke everyone up, it would only aggravate the situation.
He decided to sit down next to the bushes, where he had
hidden the bicycle hours earlier. He looked at the sky. The
stars continued to brighten the night. He thought about
his mother, deprived of all hope by medical science. He
imagined her face before her illness. Happy and full of
life. The difference was striking. Other than the stories
and the comics she read to him, she had no energy now
for any other activity. Nor was her body the same. The
most obvious was the increasing loss of her hair. It was
odd that she entrusted him to his uncle on the weekends
because on the other days she would not leave his side for
a minute. The boy thought that perhaps she was devoting
the final weekends of her life to his father. Morning
came without the boy's noticing the exact moment in
which things began to be illuminated. He sat there for an
hour longer, next to the envelope with the calculations
scribbled upon it. The note and the money he kept in his
pocket. He waited until the uncle opened the garage door
and came out with the hose to water the yard. As soon as
he saw him, the uncle's face showed his surprise. He had
believed that the boy was, at that very moment, sleeping
in the bed they made up for him on the weekends. The
boy told him that he would answer his questions later. He
went into the house without giving any explanations. The
uncle wanted to follow him, but the spray of water which
began right then made him stop. He started watering the
yard as though nothing had happened. When his father
came that afternoon to pick him up, the boy handed him
the scribbled-upon envelope, but he asked no questions

about his mother and said nothing about his visit to the delivery office or about the existence of the old woman with the crown. They went silently out to the street. The uncle looked out a window on the second floor to tell them goodbye. He waved and then disappeared into the house. After they had gone a block, the boy started talking.

Hero Dogs :

*A Look at the Future of Latin America Envisioned as an
Immobile Man and His 30 Belgian Malinois Shepherds*

Near the city's airport lives a man who, besides being an immobile man—that is, a man incapable of moving himself—is considered one of the best trainers of Belgian Malinois Shepherds in the country. He shares the house with his mother, one sister, his nurse-trainer and 30 Belgian Malinois able to kill anyone with a single bite to the jugular. No one knows why some visitors, upon entering the house where that man passes his days as a recluse, sense a link between it and what could be considered the future of Latin America. If someone asks about his condition, the man often says, in his almost incomprehensible manner of speaking, that it's one thing to be an immobile man and quite another to be mentally retarded.

In front of the house several cages are displayed. Each one contains a pair of dogs, which spend the entire day snarling at the people who pass the fence. If someone approaches, the animals react so furiously that they sometimes break teeth as they bite the bars or attack each other without pity. Each time this happens, the immobile man emits piercing whistles, prompted without a doubt by his desperation at being unable to frighten off the intruders himself. The dogs remain agitated, and the nurse-trainer has to rush out to quiet the disturbance. He uses toys able to withstand the dogs' bites and a few words in French, the official language for training Belgian Malinois.

No one knows if the nurse-trainer was nurse first, and then trainer, or vice versa–first trainer, then nurse. He is a somewhat heavy young man, whose sportswear is not quite tidy. More than once, he has shared the immobile's man's bed, especially when a deep ache tears at one of his legs.

The immobile man claims that he has not been so motionless for his whole life. He asserts that until some years ago he could turn his neck from one side to the other.

The walls of his room are painted green. From them hang various diplomas which vouch for the man's astonishing dexterity in training dogs as difficult to work with as Belgian Malinois. The immobile man is moved daily into a chair placed next to his bed. There the nurse-trainer secures the telephone receiver to his head. Behind him a hunting bird is secured; it is closed into a wooden box whenever a Belgian Malinois is brought into the room.

The immobile man owns a photo-album—which only certain people are allowed to see—with a collection of prints of the finest Belgian Malinois in the world. After making clear that it's one thing to be immobile and quite another to be mentally retarded, the immobile man asserts that there are no defective dogs, but rather stupid masters. Immediately he begins to laugh uproariously.

On the bottom floor, the mother and sister dedicate themselves to a strange labor concerned with the classification of empty plastic bags. Neither of the two seems to appreciate the entrance of strange people into the house. They show their irritation every time that someone is invited to the immobile man's room. Because he has been assigned the job of guiding the visitors, the nurse-trainer faces a troublesome situation whenever someone comes from outside. For a long time now, the immobile man has received only guests concerned with the rearing of Belgian Malinois.

At certain times of the year, the immobile man decides to get rid of one of the dogs: "Only new blood will provide the necessary genetic advances," he asserts and begins once again to laugh.

The immobile man could do without all of the dogs except Anubis. It would be easier for him to dispose of his family, the nurse-trainer or even the house itself than of his favorite animal. If he did choose the dog over the house—cruel to imagine it!—he would lie next to Anubis, at one side of the freeway that links the airport to the city. The immobile man has no doubt that his favored dog would in the most ferocious manner possible prevent anyone from nearing his supine body.

In spite of contrary opinions, principally from pseudo-specialists, the nurse-trainer does his best to persuade the visitors that the Belgian Malinois is the ideal dog for anybody with bodily difficulties. He uses the immobile man as an example, calling him—aloud and in front of the guests—a lump. He asserts that an ordinary dog would have already eaten him. The visitors listen in silence to the nurse-trainer's words. Then some of them dare to suggest that one ought not call the immobile man a lump.

The immobile man spends the greater part of the day having the dogs brought to his room. He has prepared distinct sounds for receiving them. Some of them are almost inaudible. It is curious to witness how, at the issuing of those sounds, the dogs leap, stop, bark, howl, and turn to leave the room. Some visitors, and at times even the nurse-trainer himself, are certain that the immobile man has managed to control the dogs in this manner because he has dedicated every minute of his life to observing their behavior. Once a group of intellectuals familiar with the case named the immobile man the city's most prominent dog psychologist.

The Belgian Malinois have not only established their obedience and value to the house. As the diplomas that hang from the walls certify, they have taken part in innumerable competitions, many of them international events. The dogs of the immobile man have been champions primarily of the French ring, which tests canine abilities such as tracking, the high jump, and bravery. They have likewise excelled in personal defense displays and in the detection by smell of narcotics. No one knows how, from a paralysis so absolute, the immobile man has been able to train his dogs in tests which demand such animation. The nurse-trainer seems to have an answer. Never, however, would he dare to express it in public.

One gets the impression that numerous nurse-trainers have passed through the immobile man's life, but he seems not to have developed a closer relationship than with the current one. If anyone sought to establish the age of the immobile man, he would be merely speculating. From a rapid physical observation one might deduce an age anywhere from 30 to 50 years.

It might seem peculiar to point out that, on the opposite side of the room, hangs a cage containing a half dozen Australian parakeets. Seeing them, one surrenders the idea that the bird of prey is tied by one of its claws for fear that the dogs might devour it. It seems rather that the bird is tied to preserve the lives of the parakeets.

On another wall there is a large map of Latin America where red circles mark the cities in which the rearing of Belgian Malinois is most advanced. The presence of the map leads only certain visitors to think about the future of the continent.

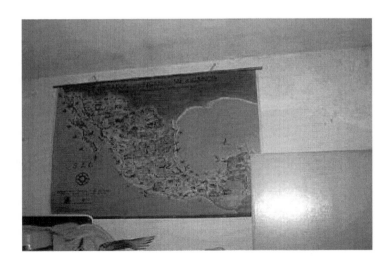

On the table where the telephone sits, the telephone whose receiver the immobile man keeps tied around his head at all times, there is a color print that shows more than a dozen space ships traversing interstellar space. The immobile man constantly asks his sister to leave her work with the plastic bags, for just a few moments, and come up to the second floor to cut some prints for him. He also asks her to insert into each one of the ships the photos of the dogs which he keeps in certain albums. The sister refuses to pay attention to him. In fact, she has never gone up to the second floor of the house they live in.

From time to time the immobile man orders the nurse-trainer to punch in the telephone number of the Reference Center. He attempts to ascertain how many Belgian Malinois could fit–in reality, not in his poster-universe–in a space ship.

There is a test which the immobile man puts the nurse-trainer through from time to time. An experiment not especially common. It begins with the immobile man asking the nurse-trainer to play, in an exaggerated fashion, with Anubis. To excite him until he feels happy. The Belgian Malinois seems quite pleased with the young man in athletic clothes, who is the only human being with whom the dog, since he was a puppy, has had actual contact. The nurse-trainer has been in charge of feeding, washing and rewarding Anubis with affection since the dog was born.

When Anubis gives the appearance of reaching an exalted state of happiness, the immobile man uses signals to order the nurse-trainer to leave the room and leave him alone with the dog. The immobile man begins then to produce the necessary sounds to make Anubis look attentively at him and, among other indications, to prick up his ears. Then he makes a noise, even more complex, advising the nurse-trainer to re-enter the room. Seeing the man enter, Anubis leaps to attack him with indescribable ferocity. The following sound, exiting the immobile man's throat, stops the dog in mid-air. In that moment the immobile man reasserts his continuing, irresistible mastery. The nurse-trainer seems to enjoy the satisfaction which the immobile man gains from the testing of Anubis.

A few minutes later, the immobile man generally orders the dialing of the number of the reference center. Apparently he wants to resolve his doubts about the relation between Belgian Malinois Shepherds and space ships. The color poster of the ships with the clipped photos of the dogs glued on top is on the table in the room. It was the nurse-trainer who used the scissors and placed the creatures where the immobile man wanted them.

So rapid is the voice which answers the phone at the reference center and so slow and distorted that which comes out of the immobile man that, in spite of the contact, the call is not at all successful. The reference center ends the call before the immobile man can pronounce his second syllable.

On the lower floor, mother and sister continue their task of classifying plastic bags. That day they expect no visitors. The dogs are all in their places. On the bottom of some of the cages there is excrement which has still not been removed. The immobile man knows it because, among other abilities, he has a highly developed sense of smell. That day, however, the situation does not seem to bother him. Some dogs will howl because their cages are not clean. Others will insistently smell their own discharges as much as the others'. Instead of worrying about the condition of the animals, the immobile man will agree that the leg which always pains him is paining him. The nurse-trainer will have to massage it. The mother and sister shout from downstairs to console him. The nurse-trainer will take advantage of that moment to ask permission of the two women to spend the night in the room.

Just before they fall asleep—together in the same bed—the immobile man hopes that they will be wakened tomorrow morning by the call from the reference center, providing the information about how many Belgian Malinois Shepherds will fit in a space ship. Waiting for the hoped-for communication to materialize, the immobile man comforts himself thinking that the circles marking the cities on the map of Latin America are, without a doubt, the locations most fit for carrying out, without difficulties, the rearing of Belgian Malinois Shepherds. The attempts carried out on other planets of the solar system likewise support this conclusion.

One could be forgiven for thinking that, there in the house of the immobile man, no one knows the circumstances in which the current nurse-trainer was hired. Certainly he is not the first to occupy the post. When the first nurse-trainer is mentioned, the immobile man cries out horribly, and the sister tries to hide under her mother's skirts. The earlier nurse-trainer appears in many photos, where one sees the immobile man competing in the rings in which he has participated. The other man is a subject with little hair who, in every instance, wears suit and tie. The immobile man insists that the earlier nurse-trainer hated the dogs, despite the fact that his principal duty was to tend to them.

The immobile man seems to have constructed his own family history. He has invented a sort of past, for each and every member of the family. Among other things, he insists that for a long time they were all secluded in various charitable institutions. That they were kept apart for close to twenty years. In order to bring them together again, the immobile man insists, the mother began a long journey when she succeeded in being discharged from the establishment where she had been kept. It was in this manner that the house began recovering its inhabitants.

When the mother appeared at the institution where the immobile man was reared, the son resisted, in every manner, being taken from the place. He asked the nurses to hide him in the storerooms at the rear. It took hours to find him. Among the strange noises he made, trying to avoid his dismissal, was something having to do with a typewriter. That was the second occasion upon which he was denied such a device. The first happened not long after he met a boy who told him that he had devoted himself to writing stories of hero dogs.

According to the account of the immobile man, the sister was a servant at the institution where he had been interned. Only so could she maintain her being there and avoid being thrown without a second thought out into the streets. As soon as the two of them were face to face, the immobile man and his sister renounced each other. They were perfectly unknown to one another.

It has never been known in what manner the immobile man secured the funds necessary to acquire the first Belgian Malinois he kept in the house. It was known only that the dogs were brought to the house by the nurse-trainer of those days. Perhaps the dogs did not cost a cent. One theory holds that this first nurse-trainer accepted the job because he had no idea what to do with the pack of dogs of which he was the owner. During the months immediately prior, fortune had turned against him. He was a trainer going through bankruptcy.

In weighing the conditions in which the family lives, many have asked themselves how they get the money to pay, not only the expenses of the dogs, but also those which human beings incur.

The current nurse-trainer came to the house with the intent of completing an academic requirement: in order to graduate as a nurse, he had first to perform a voluntary practicum. But in spite of the fact that the nurse-trainer can easily demonstrate his experience with the immobile man—and thus receive his official title—it has never occurred to him to return to the place of his training to collect the certificate.

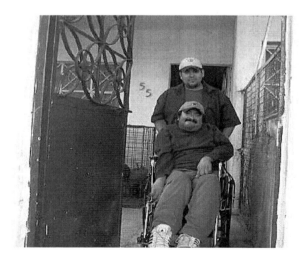

It is difficult to understand the circumstances which make it possible for the nurse-trainer to remain in the house without receiving any sort of salary. Every time the nurse-trainer brings up his decision to leave him, the immobile man silences him with the threat of ordering all of the animals killed. Hearing that, the nurse-trainer always goes down to the first floor. There, sitting with the mother and sister, he tells them he imagines a rather savage slaughter. The nurse-trainer discusses in those moments both the sort of person capable of bringing such carnage to pass and the methods he would use. The nurse-trainer believes that the executioner would be secured by means of the reference center. The mother and sister insist that, faced with such a situation, they would close themselves up, terrified, in one of the cages.

When the time of the slaughter arrives, the immobile man will ask that Anubis be the first animal sacrificed. After speaking these words, he says he feels an intense pain in the leg which hurts him so frequently. The nurse-trainer then abandons whatever he has been doing in order to begin a therapeutic massage. If the pain does not lessen, the nurse-trainer must get into the immobile man's bed, in order to warm up the painful leg with his own body. To do this, he first removes the telephone headset strapped to his head and then carries him from the chair where he spends his days to the bed beneath the cage of the Australian parakeets.

After making the immobile man comfortable beneath the bed-covers, the nurse-trainer curls up at his side. But first he descends to the first floor to ask, as usual, for permission to go to bed with the son. The immobile man and the nurse-trainer remain together until the following morning. On more than one occasion the immobile man has said that such is the only way of taking the pain away.

At one time a person, an apprentice of a canine instructor of advanced techniques was interested in acquiring one of the Belgian Malinois of the immobile man. Before giving out his address, the immobile man subjected the person to a minutely detailed examination. Via telephone he asked the other chiefly about his physical characteristics. As the immobile man's house is in a neighborhood difficult to navigate, he sent the nurse-trainer to await the apprentice at an major intersection.

The day before the arrival of the instructor's apprentice, the immobile man had decided which dogs would be offered for sale. Only those which presented the greatest difficulties would be available to the prospective buyer. One, which bit uncontrollably the first stranger to come before him, and another which displayed conduct more appropriate to a lap dog than a Belgian Malinois.

Most recently the immobile man's prestige as a trainer
of Belgian Malinois Shepherds has fallen noticeably.
Perhaps it is owing to the change in his character which
seems always more evident. Every day he shows a greater
irritability, not only with the dogs but also, even more so,
with the owners of other animals. The disdain may also
have come about because the techniques learned from the
previous nurse-trainer are already obsolete. The French
ring has developed with an astonishing rapidity. Likewise
new are collars which emit limited electric shocks so that
the dogs will obey more effectively the orders of their
trainers. In his current condition, the immobile man
has no possibility of acquiring either the collars or the
manuals already in circulation.

When the instructor's apprentice arrived at the house, the mother and sister put handkerchiefs on their heads and turned off the lights on the first floor. That day they conducted their work with the bags in the dark. Learning of the behavior of the two women, the immobile man threw himself into such a state that the mother and sister had no choice but to remove their handkerchiefs and turn the lights back on. During the visit he insulted the nurse-trainer more than once. He also did something that no one would have believed him capable of: he sacrificed, without any emotion, the hawk.

The instructor's apprentice was seated in a chair in front of the sofa. The immobile man seemed to have organized the visit to the smallest detail. To begin with, the instructor's apprentice had to remain, throughout the duration of his presence in the room, seated in that chair. The nurse-trainer had to leave the room in order to bring the dogs, one by one, from their cages. Then he had to bring them to the room. While the nurse-trainer went to retrieve each animal, the immobile man explained to the instructor's apprentice the behavior that they would display in the room. At one point the immobile man described the manner in which one of the dogs was going to kill the bird of falconry. The Belgian Malinois behaved exactly as the immobile man had predicted. When the moment came, the destruction of the raptor was quite violent.

During the display, the nurse-trainer had to maintain his silence. And so too while he brought all the Belgian Malinois Shepherds which the immobile man owned. The dogs he was interested in getting rid of were mixed in with the others. On only one occasion did one of the dogs disobey the immobile man's orders. Shakura, the oldest dog in the house, leapt unexpectedly onto the leg of the instructor's apprentice. The immobile man then berated the nurse-trainer as he had never done before. He immediately threw the innocent instructor's apprentice out of the house.

After that incident it would be impossible to carry out the necessary command training to convince someone to buy one of the dogs, the immobile man shouted from his chair.

After the instructor's apprentice left the house, the immobile man ordered the nurse-trainer to bring Shakura back to the room. The dog howled piercingly as her master castigated her.

From time to time, the mother and sister ask the nurse-trainer to help them organize the plastic bags which they have to classify every day. Neither the mother nor the sister has ever told the nurse-trainer the purpose those bags fulfill in their lives. The nurse-trainer seems, however, capable of sensing it.

Every time the mother and sister ask the nurse-trainer's assistance, the immobile man falls into a kind of nervous attack. He knows that, during those times, he will remain absolutely alone. He does not seem to count the presence of the Australian parakeets nor of the raptor in his room. In these moments, the immobile man produces the sounds necessary to make the dogs howl without stopping. It is curious how the Belgian Malinois, in spite of the distance between them, still easily hear the sounds their master produces.

Despite the conditions in which they are forced to work, with the immobile man captive to a panic attack and the dogs howling constantly, the mother and sister know that they must not give up the work they are accomplishing. The nurse-trainer is confronted in such moments with a conflict. He knows that the immobile man suffers from the abandonment of which he is the victim, but he knows as well that there are economic expenses to deal with. He works at the empty bags without thinking of the chaos set free around him. Finally neither the women nor the nurse-trainer will be able to tolerate the situation any longer and, disturbed, they will stop their work. The nurse-trainer will go up to the room and, although the immobile man does not mention his suffering, he will massage the painful leg. The mother and sister will remain hidden. The employers will not delay in coming to collect the bags and to bring others. They will have to ask, once again, for one of the customary holidays.

That night, while the immobile man sleeps, the mother and sister will work twice as hard as usual. During such times the Belgian Malinois generally remain calm, as long as the immobile man has not requested that Anubis spend the night at his side. The other dogs, sensing that Anubis is the one watching him that night, will stir restlessly until dawn.

On these nights the nurse-trainer will be forced, over and over again, to give up his work with the bags in order to go to the cages. In spite of his efforts, however, he will not be able to pacify the dogs completely. The Belgian Malinois will only calm down with the first light of dawn. Then the nurse-trainer will go up to the second floor to take the immobile man a cup of tea. The nurse-trainer knows that he cannot, at these times, enter the room without notice. He must knock first, discreetly, making sure the immobile man is awake and has given the necessary instructions so that Anubis will not tear him to pieces as soon as he sees him entering with the cup. On mornings of this kind, it is most likely that the immobile man will feign sleep. No matter how much he might hear, not only the knocks at the door but also the tender words of the nurse-trainer, he will pretend to perceive nothing.

The mother and sister will listen with anguish from the lower floor to the devious awakening of the immobile man. They will insist, urgently, that the nurse-trainer return to the first floor and continue helping them with the work. Neither the mother nor the sister knows, to tell the truth, what to do with the plastic bags they have to classify. They are limited to placing them in piles, over and again. While the immobile man refuses to answer and continues pretending to sleep, they can make little progress. It isn't that they don't love the immobile man and earnestly desire that he wake up and drink the hot tea. They even enjoy the tone of voice with which the nurse-trainer, carefully holding the cup, announces the arrival of the new day.

Anubis remains silent. His ears, on the other hand, demonstrate his alertness. He seems to be awaiting the order to take action. The immobile man suddenly opens one eye. Following his custom, he will open the other one ten minutes later. Perhaps he could continue enjoying that game indefinitely. Opening and closing the eyes without stopping. He knows the others are hanging by a thread. He knows as well that they think, although they are incapable of expressing it, that he might even be dead.

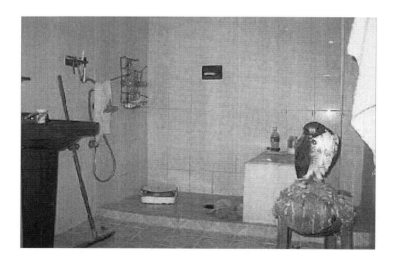

In the event that the immobile man were nothing more than a cadaver, it would require an act of real prowess to collect the body. Anubis would give his life before allowing anyone to put one finger on the inert body of his master. It is hunger, which the immobile man begins to feel, which always brings the situation to an end. His stomach grumbles softly. He hasn't had a bite since six p.m. of the day before. At that hour the nurse-trainer brought him something light. The nurse-trainer concludes his procedure for waking the immobile man by offering, along with the cup of tea, a sandwich which, he makes clear, he will prepare immediately. Only then will the immobile man make a noise, however minimal. Anubis will howl in accompaniment to his master's sounds. Downstairs the mother and sister will not be able to restrain themselves and will laugh furtively. The nurse-trainer enters the room then in order to leave the cup of tea on the night table. Anubis growls softly. He does not attack, however, because the slight noise produced by the immobile man's throat was an order to keep him quiet.

The nurse-trainer leaves the room seconds later. With a sort of desperation he goes downstairs. The possibility of tripping and falling does not seem to matter to him. Running he passes the mother and sister who, full of hope, look at him. Before returning to sit with them, he will have to go to the kitchen to prepare the promised sandwich. Dawn still has not come. Far off they hear the rumbling of the cars which come and go from the airport.

According to the immobile man, he was taken after his birth to a charitable institution so that he might receive the necessary rearing. Taking into account the characteristics of the infant before them, a number of scientists did not believe the mother prepared for a maternal responsibility of that nature. The immobile man is clear that, as soon as she was released from the hospital where he was born, the mother returned home alone with the less than noble intention of suffocating her older child. At that time the home consisted of only one room. The immobile man's sister was saved at the last moment from that homicidal fit. Some of the neighbors—who rushed out to welcome the mother, to meet the new baby, and to return the daughter which the mother had left with them during her stay in the hospital—testified to the uncontrolled exaltation of the woman. Quite nonchalantly, and without even allowing the neighbors time to return home, she placed a pillow over the face of the terrified child. Post-partum depression was the diagnosis of the same scientists who, days earlier, had taken guardianship of the newborn son.

According to the immobile man's usual account, the mother was secluded at the bidding of the neighbors. At first it seems that no institution wanted to admit her. She had to try to set fire to her home, a week after the attempted murder, before the authorities intervened again. This is one of the versions which the immobile man repeats most often. It seems that, by telling these stories over and again, he seeks to explain the reasons why, supposedly, he did not grow up in what might be called a typical nuclear family.

For about twenty years, the members of the family were kept apart. From the beginning the sister missed the mother to an incalculable degree. She never got used to the separation. That may be the reason that she lost, in a relatively short time, a good part of her teeth. Her eyebrows and lashes, on the other hand, fell out gradually. The immobile man asserts—and doing so he causes the sister, if she hears him, to give in to irritable outbursts difficult to deal with—that during his years of internment he was treated like royalty. He declares that he had at his disposal the entire time three nurses whom he asked every day for the clipped photograph of one dog or another. At that time he still showed no particular predilection for any particular breed. He kept around his bed a series of figures of spaniels, dachshunds, setters, and bigger dogs. Some of the figures were glued to the walls. Others were piled up in a drawer of a small dresser of the sort given to all the children in the institution.

During those years he met a boy who said he had written a book about dogs with heroic lives. The boy had illustrated the book with clipped images, much like those multiplying around his bed. The boy writer came to the ward for a visit during the month of October, 1967. He had just, that very morning, had first communion. The parish had organized the mission of mercy. Days before, those responsible had notified the parents that there would be no visits to the wards of children with infectious illnesses. The pilgrimage would include only the wards of the burn victims or of those with psychomotor problems.

It seems that the boy writer was particularly drawn to a patient who was missing a part of his nose. Perhaps for that reason he turned over the entire contents of the bag of gifts that he brought with him. It carried two dozen surprises, wrapped in colored paper. According to the account the immobile man always gives, when the boy saw the cut-out images of the dogs on the walls of the sanatorium, he asserted that he was a writer and had composed a book about hero dogs. He said also that, once he finished it, no one but his grandmother had been interested in reading it.

That same afternoon the immobile man asked, for the first time in his life, for a typewriter. He requested it from the nurses who watched out for his well-being. Just like the other boy, he wanted to write a series of stories. He had already imagined the stories while he looked at the pictures that they cut out for him every day. He asked again for a typewriter only when he was released from the institution.

Sometimes the immobile man tells the nurse-trainer stories concerning the thirty Belgian Malinois Shepherds he keeps at the house, and about the raptor which had to be covered with a wooden box every time the dogs entered the room. On occasion he even speaks of the Australian parakeets. While he structures those tales—in a slow, confused way—the immobile man forgets that his mother and sister work on the lower floor with the bags which they are always late in delivering. They take advantage of any time when the immobile man is enjoying himself to call for the nurse-trainer—who often leaves the room without the immobile man even noticing—and push forward urgently on the work they have been entrusted with. Both remember always that it was exactly these plastic bags which brought the family together again. The nurse-trainer frequently attempts to discover how precisely those bags could be the instrument which succeeded in reuniting them.

In spite of the fact that the nurse-trainer knows that the matter of the family members' reclusion in separate institutions is a sham, he behaves as though that period in the life of the house's inhabitants were true. When he asks the women about the family's past, he does nothing but inspire a respectful silence. Both of them are convinced that such a state, in which enforced silence creates tension of a sort, produces the best conditions for their labor. For that reason, and surely in order to increase their output, the mother and sister constantly provoke the nurse-trainer to ask them how plastic bags could possibly have brought them together. The silence ends when, on the second floor, the immobile man, giving off his usual sounds, incites a chain reaction of barking which involves all thirty of the Belgian Malinois Shepherds kept in the house. In these situations the nurse-trainer goes immediately up the stairs.

Every day the immobile man tells the nurse-trainer that he would like to converse again with the boy who, forty years earlier, told him that he had written a book about hero dogs. That memory makes him forget, with increasing frequency, the existing relationship between the Belgian Malinois and spaceships. He even forgets the map of Latin America which continues to hang on one of the walls of the room. The immobile man often tells the nurse-trainer that he wants to talk to the boy at six p.m., the exact time at which he left the hospital ward where the immobile man was being housed. At times his longing becomes rather excited. Then the nurse-trainer tries various ways to calm his anxiety. The most common is to bring all of the dogs to the room. Each one of the Belgian Malinois has an established time to remain there. The average per animal is about ten minutes. When this sort of situation arises, the nurse-trainer spends some four hours at the task. Before bringing in the first dog, the nurse-trainer has to place the wooden box over the hunting bird. At these times the Australian parakeets generally find themselves covered with a blanket printed with the solar system.

Even though the nurse-trainer has never forgotten, the immobile man always reminds him—in most cases with excited cries—to put the wooden box over the hawk before bringing the dogs to the room. He gives the order even when the bird is no longer in the room. Only after the last Belgian Malinois visited the room did the nurse-trainer turn to the vital necessities of that bird. When the hawk had not yet been torn to pieces, the nurse-trainer would go then to the first floor and take from a jar one of the living mice he tended as food for the bird. He generally kept a half dozen of them, replenishing the supply once a week with rodents he bought in the market. The nurse-trainer would introduce the mouse, hidden in a device the immobile man had christened the rodent transport. It was a small tube of metallic mesh which featured a handle on the top. Once he had returned to the room, the nurse-trainer would uncover the birdcage and unbind the bird's foot. Then he would open the door of the carrier and harry the mouse to make it run out. The chaos unleashed in the room every time the bird threw himself into the hunt was indescribable. Oddly enough these times, when the bird rampaged into everything around him, were among the few when the immobile man laughed, in a distinctive manner which everyone knew. His smile could in some way have been considered beatific.

Meanwhile, and because of the events just transpired, on the lower floor the mother and sister covered their heads with two of the plastic bags. Then they left the house. Apparently they could not tolerate the commotion when the bird set upon the mouse.

From the window of the second floor, the nurse-trainer watched the two women drawing away. In such moments he was never sure if they would return. But think about it: the immobile man continues smiling with no change at all.

My Skin Luminous

*. . . in the neighborhood of the tomb
of the holy Sufi Nizamudin*

During the time that I lived with my mother, it never occurred to me that accommodating my genitals in her presence might have a significant repercussion. I was wrong. Later I learned that she even asked the other women for objects of value in exchange for a full look at them. Adjusted, stricken, on the verge of exploding. My mother taking advantage of my suffering. Tirelessly gathering up objects. In many cases things to eat or little articles of jewelry: plastic rings or a slender cord she hung on her wrist. Once she got a pencil she used to paint her lips. Delineating her mouth seemed to give her such excitement that she forgot about my presence for several moments. Then I managed to untie the strange garment which she thought up for our trips to the public baths. I was completely unclothed. A diffuse light illuminated my flesh. I decided to throw myself into the water. Into the deepest part. I moved aside several obese women whose bodies impeded my passage. I was at the point, even, of crossing into the men's section. If I had managed that, I am sure that my mother would never have dealt with me in the same manner again. I found myself on all four. The water was mixed with mud. If I had stood up, it would have come barely to my ankles. I would then be exposed all over again to the looks which make it possible for me to enter these baths today. The woman would poke into their belongings and arrange, by means of the exchange as particular as my body itself, to contemplate me as long as they considered necessary. Unexpectedly it occurred to me to turn. My mother was lingering next to the basins of thermal waters. She was still distracted by the rite of decorating her mouth. The others watched her attentively, except for the overweight women who seemed desperate to leave the area reserved for them. I am bold enough to say that that scene, of my mother painting her lips, was a display sufficiently foreign to the customs of the region. It seemed, to me, so far beyond our normal practices that I could not contain myself, and I shouted. My voice grew louder and louder. The rebounding of the water against the concrete channels made the words I was throwing at her reverberate. I could not stand for my mother's mouth to become more of a spectacle than that my testicles are able to offer. But at the moment it seemed to be so. Even the obese women seemed disposed to break the rules and were preparing to make their way into the section where the thermal waters were. Such a thing had never happened before. From a certain age and depending upon the qualities of each body, everyone has an assigned area. Only children and adolescents are permitted to go from one area to another without anyone's approval. In earlier times it was the custom to remain in the water for a number of hours. At that time I had not yet experienced how detrimental excess often is. I was still unaware of the ancient remains exposed in newer surfaces when liquid substances wash over them again and again. Discerning the marks which time produces in those textures is perhaps one of the most important lessons to be learned about these public baths. Only my testicles, always disposed for exhibition, seem to escape this type of constant decay. My mother would generally wait for me at the exit. She was obviously pleased when we met up again, and she almost always carried the things she had collected during the day. Most of the gifts offered her as an exchange pleased her, but she seemed to have begun to feel a special predilection for lipstick pencils. More than once she woke me at dawn in order to show off her mouth tinted purple or phosphorescent fuchsia. It was difficult for me to be sure if that excited figure was part of a dream or part of something that truly existed. Usually my mother would continue showing me her lips until I was completely awake. Dawns like those make it difficult to return to a restful sleep. I remain instead between sleep and waking. On those occasions I play an old game—one which has entertained me since childhood—which consists of removing my genitals, without the use of my hands, from the unusual underwear my mother makes for me. This garb, which I have to wear all of the time though I rarely pay any attention to it, is not truly her own invention. In designing it she has followed a series of patterns of ancient date. Besides that, I know that the role of a mother who has dedicated herself to the display of her sons' genitals is likewise not her invention. It is a millenary practice which not all mothers of sons are able to take part in. In actuality almost none can be found to carry out an exercise of this nature. Thus the miniscule number of mothers of this type which exist today. In the province in which we live the existence of another such woman had never been known. It must have been my own mother who told everyone that, about fifty years earlier, her grandmother's sister had become, by means of this office, the most powerful woman in her natal home. There was still some memory of her activities, but not even my mother knew what finally happened to her or, more to the point, to the son who had brought her such prestige. "What they say is true," my mother told me one of those early mornings when she woke me to show me her lips covered with an oily patina. "People remember a great deal about the women who display the genitals but nothing about the sons put on exhibition." Then I knew that the boys were killed mercilessly. I fell into a deep sleep, full of dreams which continued in the following nights. I imagined the bearing of the women who enriched themselves by offering these spectacles, and that of the sons themselves. They say that the genitals at last fall prey to the sickness which propitiates the envy of the others, that between one moment and the next they begin to dry up until the inflated sack that contained them is no more than a lean, dangling tripe that finally drops from the body before the victim notices what is happening. When the sons lose their testicles in that fashion, the mothers flee immediately. They carry as much of their accumulated possessions as they can and, most often, turn toward the mountainous regions. Long ago the law laid out the procedure by which those boys had to die. One of the most frequently employed methods was to withhold treatment from the wounded scrotum. I learned of that procedure only recently. The headmistress of the Special School I attended described it to me. "Why am I now enrolled in a Special School?" I ask myself constantly. I believe that no one, not even one of my likewise secluded fellows, has a definite answer. They accept, as I do, knowing that I sleep in one of the central wards. My mother might know since she had insisted so strongly that the headmistress accept me. My repeated exposures in the public baths did not seem to be enough. Enriching herself with the things she continued to acquire. Painting her lips to the point of satiety. The impression was that all of that was little enough. Anyone who had seen her at that time would think that she hated me with her whole heart. Indeed if they had witnessed the joy on her face when the headmistress finally gave her verdict, they would find that the only explanation. When the desire that I be a part of the Special School was born in my mother, we were already visiting the baths regularly. At that time such a school was perhaps the only avenue she could find in order to be considered a more or less normal mother in our community. It was perhaps a manner of overcoming my father's abandonment of his family. My father's lover had died, not long before, of a serious illness. She had been employed as a secretary in the public institution where he worked. I never knew if she was his secretary or simply another employee. What truly stood out to me was that my mother suffered that woman's illness as if it had been developing in her own body. It was some time after we had been abandoned—my father left us one winter morning—that my mother began to undertake a series of experiments with my body. I suppose the purpose was to make my admittance into the Special School more certain. In those days we were living once again in the storeroom of my grandfather's cookery. Among other actions, she gave me a pair of glasses which transformed the real world into an unrecognizable presence, good only for making me disagreeably nauseous. On other occasions she would not let me breathe, covering my face with a pillow until I thought I would die. Once she tried to place my head into a skull which she kept for who knows what purpose. Another morning, when she found me buying candies with money that had fallen from a boy's pocket into the street, she scorched my hands in a fire she lit with the sole proposition of teaching me my lesson. My mother at last secured my entry into the Special School after the first outing we made to the public baths. Someone had told her that such a visit was the only way to get the headmistress to give her consent. My mother was a truly poor woman then. She did not even have the purse which she now shows off enthusiastically. We were living alone in the storeroom of the cookery where my grandfather has always baked the community's swine. Our bodies began to give off a smell that became a stench. My mother had been saving up in order to pay for our admittance to the baths, because in those days an expense like that was an almost unattainable enterprise. Because we supposed that the visit was at hand, we decided to give up immediately the methods of cleanliness we normally practiced. We had to economize in every way. No buying water from the men who came door to door. No bags of the soap which some of the local businessmen sold on the main street, soap which had not been completely used up in the public baths. When we had finally collected the price of entrance, we got up before the sun rose. We quickly left the storeroom. We knew that the lines of those waiting to go inside formed early. Many were businesspeople who went to the baths before beginning their day's work. There were also women of the highest ancestry who apparently wanted to take advantage of the opaque light of dawn so that no one could get a close glimpse of their bodies before they introduced themselves into the water. On that first visit we stayed for a number of hours. The gifts began to appear as soon as my mother had removed my pants. From then on we were allowed into the baths without paying. We bustled in whenever we could. For that reason my body never again held that disagreeable smell. My skin changed in only a few weeks. Without anyone's notice it came to have a kind of patina, somewhat viscous, and a luminosity which is, for some, more astounding than my genitals themselves. I never asked my mother what she thought of that fact. I believe that doing so would have been an invitation for her to discover new possibilities for my body. I do not even want to think about the power that a luminous skin would have been able to grant her. She would have conceived of some manner of enclosing me in a hermitage which she would have ordered built in the vicinity of the saint's tomb where the baths were allegedly located. She would fill the space with flowers and candles and would also make sure there was a strolling musician to play some instrument capable of giving an ambience to the scene. She would not permit anyone to touch me, to put a finger to my skin. It would be—exactly like the original nature of the exercise of displaying me tirelessly—an activity of a strictly visual order. It occurs to me that it would be no different than dusting my flesh with a fistful of the diamantine we used in the Special School to carry out some of our tasks. Every week the teacher assigns us the obligation to carry out a manual task which we have to turn in, adorned with a coating of shining powder. Thus it was I began to design domestic lamps, paper ash-trays, bottles of various shapes, whose surfaces were always covered with the glaze formed by mixing diamantine with soap-foam which, according to the teachers, provides the true body of these objects. These are among the few memories I keep of my school years. Although it is, to a certain point, strange to consider as memories things which have just happened. Still, though there are few people who will believe it, I continue my attendance there. It can be said that I am one of the boarding students. I do not understand the reasoning: as if I am someone kept from going out to the street, supposing I have the time, or—to phrase it better—the requisite permission to spend entire days in the baths where my mother is tirelessly dedicated to displaying me to the other women of the area. The ward I sleep in can be considered the largest in the institution. When day has not yet completely declared itself, my mother often enters, trying to make the least possible noise. In order not to disturb the particular silence of those hours, she customarily presents herself in a rather curious manner. She arches her body in such a way as to transform it into an almost abnormal being. In the baths I have often seen bodies like that which my mother assumes in her attempt to move without sound. I have noticed that these anomalies result from different causes. I know, for example, that the contact of certain organisms with the environment produces physical alterations difficult to understand. I am continually exposed to exaggeratedly robust bodies and, on the other hand, to those whose skeletons seem barely to support them. Until very recently I did not really think of my mother as a physical being. She was distinguished from other women only by the color of her lips. The single important mark was her daubed mouth, not the contortions she sustains in search of silence. Now, after having experienced so much, I do not know what to think of my mother's body when I see her come in during the night with the key which the headmistress of the Special School seemed to have entrusted to her from the time of my admittance. The key is long and somewhat rusted. My mother's ability to come into the ward without attracting any attention is astonishing. At times, as strange as it might sound, the effort she puts forth to contort her body puts shallow cracks into the carmine of her lips. I never dared to tell her openly, but I prefer her mouth when it looks like that, with its brilliance somewhat lackluster. She almost always waits until she has totally aroused me before reapplying the lipstick. On those occasions it seems as though she is ashamed to do so. Undertaking the operation she abandons the irregular posture she so often adopts and leans over the side of my bed. But her entrance to the ward is not always realized in absolute silence. More than once, especially when she was just uncovering the potential of the pencils, my mother was imbued with a kind of frenzy as she imprinted her lips above me, making such intense noises in her throat that I irremediably ended up with an erection I attempted to contain within the rough cloth my own mother has designed for me. To this very day I appreciate the consideration she shows toward others when she daubs her lips without drawing the attention of anyone else. It would have been terrible if she wakened the other boarders. Apparently she senses that she can only get something from me by acting in silence. "How does she manage to get in here?" I ask myself every time I see her appear in the darkness. I mentioned that she comes in with the key the school's headmistress has turned over to her. And yet that proposition seems completely absurd to me. It is impossible that the headmistress would have given her a key. Perhaps she gives some of the things she collects in the baths to the monitors so that they will let her in. Or maybe she succeeds at coming in by shamelessly displaying her decorated lips. I imagine that she moves them in such a fashion that there is no choice but to stand aside. Once I am completely awake we, likewise in silence, leave the ward. I am certain the headmistress has no idea about our flights. It seems obvious to me that such a strict woman believes I am sleeping all night in the bed assigned to me.

I see the other boarders again only at bedtime, when I return after the daily visits to the baths. I also see them on Sunday because then my mother, surely in order to sleep longer than usual, gives me free rein. Her Sunday torpor never ceased to surprise me. It is an effort for me to believe that she prefers to remain in bed, on those days precisely when she could be collecting objects in a greater number than usual. Sundays are truly fruitful work days, especially at nightfall when some characters like to undertake, almost as though in secret, a fortuitous stroll. The majority of these will be women who have not married or men of varying degrees of femininity, those who choose Sunday's waning hours to visit the facilities. From time to time lovers who have been suddenly abandoned, who tend to take refuge along a certain aqueduct, or those afflicted with contagious diseases also come out. There is such desperation in many of those who appear on those days that without fail they arrive carrying gifts of the most diverse provenance. They hurry along with bags full of things which I imagine will have taken them days to gather up. I know all of this because of a memorable Sunday when my mother decided not to sleep the day away. Now, though, it is apparent that her rest is essential. Before leaving for the baths I usually look at my companions in the ward, all of them sleeping as though nothing out of the ordinary were occurring. "Are they dreaming?" I ask myself. I had just learned—I believe it was the headmistress herself who told me—that I would still have to remain a resident at the school for some time. There is nothing I lack. I believe that, between my boarding at the school and the visits to the baths, I have more than enough. It seems to me that neither memory of my father nor any nostalgia over my grandfather's cookery matters. I believe that my residence in the school will last as long as an eternity. For this reason I will know every corner of its facilities, the least details of the character of the boarders, even the profound nature of the minds of the teachers and of the headmistress herself. Only now do I realize that, in the Special School, my testicles have no reason to exist. In these wards no one has the inclination to hand over anything, neither to my mother nor to me, for the spectacle which they are able to offer. Will there be others boarded in the Special School? Although I do not know, I suspect so. And yet I feel that this is something I am not ignorant of, because I have even affirmed it more than once. I have always said that I rely on my companions in reclusion. I have no assurance, however, that many other things, apparently more important, are certain, not simply among my companions at this time but also especially in my private life. I do not know, for example, the number of siblings I have had. I have forgotten as well what my father looks like. Perhaps asking my mother would dispel the doubts. But at this point it is absurd to put it to her directly. It is most likely that she would use one of her pencils to hide herself and show me her face painted with the strangest colors imaginable. After my father's departure, I never heard my mother say anything sensible. Before, I had to follow her all the time. We went together through the streets, the parks; we walked in front of the houses of those accustomed, particularly during the holidays, to bringing their pigs to be prepared in my grandfather's cookery. We rode the public buses and, more than once, stopped to have a drink on one of the corners. I accompanied her as well in going through the procedures of the Special School and, as the reader knows, on the first excursion to the public baths. Only the glow of my skin and, of course, the firmness of the pouch which contains my testicles create the appearance that my body maintains its youth. Once, quite early in the morning, I looked, from the window of the ward in which I sleep, at the playground. The little slide, the empty swings. The sun had yet to rise. Almost immediately I felt my mother's hand on my shoulder. It was getting late. I noticed at once that, on this occasion, she appeared without the purse which she is never separated from. There was no make-up on her face, as in earlier times, when the whole family lived together in the vicinity. We resided there for many years; it was before my mother and I moved into the storeroom at my grandfather's cookery, where she had spent her childhood and youth. I remember the narrow hallways of the place, the parking lots for the neighbors' vehicles, the business district. It is not my habit to relay this information. I do not like to speak of the years in which my father, my mother, my siblings and I formed part of an actual family. At first the house was rented to us for a couple of years; I remember it as a marvelous moment. With my father, my mother and my siblings making plans for a better future. Still without the least consciousness of my testicles which, at that time, were so miniscule that I prefer not to mention them. Once the rental term was completed, the owner began to visit us every night. He asked us to vacate the property as soon as possible. The agreed term had ended, he told us repeatedly. I am not sure, besides, if my father paid the rent promptly or not. I do not know if that was an additional reason cited by the owner in his demand. In that period my father was employed at a government agency. He left the house every day, heading off to work. He went in a publicly owned car, which crossed the city from one extreme to the other. The beauty of his white shirts especially caught my attention. In some fashion my mother succeeded, years later, in bringing that brilliance over into the clothing she designed to hold my testicles. But unlike the underwear I use today, which get dirty so quickly because of the constant activity, my father's shirts resisted soiling the whole day. Once in his office he must have put on plastic sleeve-protectors to prevent the fabric from wearing out in the daily routine. There was a time during which, here in the baths, my mother refused to accept any sort of gift. I believe it happened when she ceased utilizing her purse regularly. During those days she did not want to receive either clothing or cords to tie around her wrist. She began offering the spectacle of my testicles in a gratuitous manner. It seemed rather strange to me that there was no remuneration at all. I did not like that situation. I was convinced that my genitals had to provide some sort of satisfaction to my mother at all times. This sudden necessity not to charge a fee appeared early one morning when I questioned her about her pregnancies during the years we all lived together as a family, when I asked her about the time before we moved to the storeroom of my grandfather's cookery. I wanted, like any child, to know if I had siblings. But I do not want to speak, neither of the years we lived as a family nor of the time we took refuge in the storeroom of the cookery. Nor of the reasons why the question about the pregnancies made my mother decide not to accept gifts in exchange for the observation of my testicles. The house, as I have said, had been rented to us for two years. I insist in believing, however, that asking my mother might have resolved many of my doubts. At times I need to know if the contract for the house was really for that length of time. Although if I stop and think, I consider it progressively more absurd to turn to her. Will she really be able to listen attentively to someone? More than once I have seen her take foolish pride in the youth of the pouch in which my testicles abide. She often examines it with great care. Terrified, I imagine, before the possibility of the slightest marker of withering. When my mother ausculates me, I take notice in her face of certain features like my grandfather's, he who cooked the swine. They say he died cut up into little pieces. It all began with the diabetes that required them to deprive him one leg first. My mother always tended to him. It was an insuperable occasion in which to denounce destiny the livelong day. At that time she was still a single woman. Shortly thereafter it was necessary to remove the other leg. Both arms followed. My grandfather never stopped looking at the image, hanging on the wall, of the venerated Duce, Benito Mussolini, which was kept during this whole time as a witness to the experience. More than once I heard my mother say that my grandfather, during his youth, had been part of the Urban Brigades. When this happens, when I begin to imagine familial resemblances in my mother's face, I prefer to turn my back and look out the window of the ward. Then I see once again the playground. I remain contemplating the little slide, the stopped swings. I maintain my stasis until I again feel my mother, intent on returning me quickly from my state of contemplation, putting her hand on my shoulder. It is then, with the vision of the abandoned playground as a background, that I remember the first moments of my testicles, when they began to be a part of my reality. It was during the time that my father's secretary becam gravely ill. Every evening our father sat us at the table in the kitchen and, while we had our supper, he gave us a detailed recounting of the condition of the dying woman. "I am not going to leave this house until they produce a court order," my father said in a convincing way at sunset on the day he had decided not to continue talking about his secretary. It seems that the matter of the eviction from the house was threatening. The property owner's visits provoked in me a series of feverish states which lasted the remainder of the night. Was it then I began to be aware of my genitals? The fever created images in my head which would transform themselves into uncommon shapes. I believe it was then that I imagined that we found ourselves in the baths located next to the tomb of a saint. Furthermore, of an unknown faith. Nizamudin, Nizamudin, I heard more than once in the midst of the darkness. At such moments I called from my bed for my mother who almost never paid any attention to me, busy as she was in attending to her husband. I wanted to tell her that I could not go on under the oppression that such presences caused me, nor that of the voices sounding out of nothing. On nights like those I had a sort of premonition. I saw myself submerged in wet surfaces, dragging those enormous genitals and asking naked men about the health of my father's secretary.

That woman was kept in the hospital for months. I am sure that those days, during which an eviction order was hanging over our house, are marked by the illness which carried her into death. There were constant references to complicated treatments of dialysis, to indestructible viruses, to the youth and the fortitude of the sick woman. My mother seemed to be the most affected by the situation. She was so disturbed that, during our breakfasts, she would speak of nothing but the unfortunate woman. From dawn on she would repeat, again and again, that her husband's lover was condemned to death. In that time the word lover irritated me. Now I believe it would not do so. I have even forgotten, here in the baths, its true significance. Every day, after returning from work, my father gave us a rapid update on the situation. My mother listened attentively. Then she put her hands on her husband's shoulders. She remained there, just behind the man who was master of the table. Remembering them in that pose, my uncertainty about the actual number of members of my family returns. Above all I cannot remember my siblings; they are not present in any family scene. It would be easy to ask. But I prefer to remain quiet. It no longer matters to me to know any other detail of those years. Although indeed I want to preserve the picture of that couple at the table, worried about the reports from the hospital. When my father left the house—he left one morning for the funeral of his secretary and did not return—my mother remained closed up in our home for several months. Do not think that she was following the normal routine of a housewife. She remained motionless in one of the kitchen chairs. Without thought, I am sure. The promised eviction order, which came suddenly, seemed to arouse her. Not many hours later, several men carried our things to the street. It was strange to look at the beds, the wardrobes and the chairs placed in the middle of the sidewalk. Neighbors approached. More than one of them said it was the first time such a thing had happened in the domestic accommodations. Several charitable persons, who aimed to keep her a prudent distance from the work of those taking everything from the house, took my mother to a park. My siblings—now I understand that indeed I had siblings—began to cry desperately. Other people, surely kinder than the first group, took them into their houses. Before his secretary's illness, my father sang and played the guitar. When that happened, we all gathered in the living room. The celebrations stopped suddenly. My father had sung and played the guitar even when the owner threatened to throw us out of the house from one minute to the next. As will be supposed from what I have related, the atmosphere had become somber. Some afternoons I saw my mother weeping and complaining of how unjust life can be for the needy. I never knew whom she was referring to: whether to her own father, or to herself, or to the dying woman. Now I know that she was speaking of me. That the omens about me which she had surely already begun to glimpse tormented her. On the other hand, when I think seriously about it I believe that she was exaggerating in her understandings. That I was not—nor am I now—the person indicated to represent her sorrows. As we already know, the secretary died. My father disappeared forever. I do not believe that my mother could be happy, in spite of the leather purse she always takes with her, the make-up pencils, and the ribbons which, from time to time, she ties around her wrists. For the past several days a thought, more precisely an uneasiness, pursues me. I do not know how to tell my mother that soon she will cease to receive the amount of gifts she has become accustomed to. I have a presentiment that this situation, of showing my body in exchange for receiving objects, will end at any moment. That it will terminate, in spite of the delight that the spectacle I am able to offer continues to produce. Until now everyone seems to think it impossible that my luminous skin might dull at some point. That my testicles will fail to appear powerful. They do not know that I have already begun to experience sensations which, soon or late, will render my genitals heavy and fetid. Precisely because no one suspects it, I am certain that the transformation will be obvious before long. As surely as that ancestor of mine experienced it, the one whose own mother killed him before she fled to the mountains, I begin to feel the subtle lengthening of my scrotum. It seems to follow an invisible path toward the earth. Although it happens with the requisite watchfulness to insure that its decay takes place as a great secret. When I expect it least, it will become nothing more than a useless scrap. When that point arrives, I know that my mother will not hesitate even an instant. She will cut it off with a single slash. Then she will place upon the wound a series of substances capable of creating a rapid infection in me. I have no doubt that she will act with the decisiveness characteristic of her. After, she will surely experience a state of temporal dementia similar to that in which my father's abandonment submerged her, which left her seated in a chair for entire days. She will remember, I am sure, the splendid times at my grandfather's swine cookery. When she was a single woman and, along with her father, operated a prosperous business. Those two were the only members of the family to survive the war. My mother was in charge of adorning the cuts people left for cooking. Perhaps foreseeing that ability, she was baptized with the same name as Mussolini's daughter. She placed on the cuts small ear-rings, diadems or metal hoops, so that one pig would not be confused with another as they were cooked. She will act, I am sure, wielding the firmness of character with which she attempted to convert me into the principal attraction of the tomb of the saint, Nizamudin, in whose neighborhood we now seem to find ourselves. Two nights ago my mother brought me some photos which, at first, seemed to me newly taken. Their subject was someone dedicated, like my grandfather, to the position of baker of swine. In the photo I was able to recognize the walls, the tables of cement, the long shovel my grandfather habitually used to complete his work. I could also see, over the bodies, adornments similar to those my mother placed in the animals' flesh so that they could be recognized afterward by their owners. They were trinkets of little value, not like the things I make with diamantine at the Special School. My mother and the headmistress always say that my talent is nothing special. I have learned nothing more of my father, although surely he would have appreciated like no one else my lamps covered with soap suds.

MARIO BELLATIN

(Mexico, 1960) has published such acclaimed novellas as *Flores*, which received the 2000 Xavier Villaurrutia Prize, and *Salón de belleza*, whose French translation was a finalist for the 2000 Medicis Prize for best foreign novel. His many other works include *Canon perpetuo* and *Jacobo el mutante*. His work has also been translated into German. *Chinese Checkers: Three Fictions* is his first book to appear in English.

Cooper Renner edits the online literary magazine *elimae* (elimae.com) and publishes poetry under the name Cooper Esteban. His collection, tentatively entitled *Mosefolket*, is upcoming from Ravenna Press.